"I'll back off on inserting my opinions," Olivia promised. "Provided I still have a job."

Jack's lip twitched, as if he were about to crack a smile. "I haven't fired anyone. *Yet.*"

Jack stared at her. He leaned back, rubbing his thumb and forefinger along his lower lip, studying her in that calculating way of his. Shook his head. Leaned forward, steepled his hands and released a breath before raking all ten fingers through his buzz, which looked more light brown than dark blond, as it had in Sully's photos. "You are one stubborn broad."

She burst out laughing because he'd muttered it mostly to himself. And because it was true.

His eyes lit at her laughter and for a moment she felt frozen in time. He was drop-dead gorgeous even when he scowled like his father, but with his finely chiseled face all loose in laughter like that, he was finer than fine.

She needed to shore up her resistance. She couldn't be attracted to him. That enamoredness would fade soon. It had to. Trusting was too dangerous a journey to embark on.

USA TODAY bestselling author and RN **Cheryl Wyatt** writes romance with virtue themed with rescue. She's a grateful worshipper of Jesus. She's also a mom, a wife, and a wrangler of words and spoiled Yorkies. She loves readers and cherishes interaction at facebook.com/cherylwyattauthor or through email at cheryl@cherylwyatt.com. View her book list and join her newsletter at cherylwyatt.com.

The Hero's Sweetheart

Cheryl Wyatt

HARLEQUIN® LOVE INSPIRED®

Recycling programs
for this product may
not exist in your area.

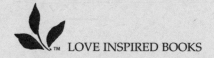 LOVE INSPIRED BOOKS

ISBN-13: 978-0-373-71937-2

The Hero's Sweetheart

Copyright © 2016 by Cheryl Wyatt

All rights reserved. Except for use in any review, the reproduction
or utilization of this work in whole or in part in any form by any
electronic, mechanical or other means, now known or hereinafter
invented, including xerography, photocopying and recording, or in
any information storage or retrieval system, is forbidden without
the written permission of the editorial office, Love Inspired Books,
233 Broadway, New York, NY 10279 U.S.A.

This is a work of fiction. Names, characters, places and incidents are
either the product of the author's imagination or are used fictitiously, and
any resemblance to actual persons, living or dead, business establishments,
events or locales is entirely coincidental.

This edition published by arrangement with Love Inspired Books.

® and TM are trademarks of Love Inspired Books, used under license.
Trademarks indicated with ® are registered in the United States Patent
and Trademark Office, the Canadian Intellectual Property Office and in
other countries.

www.Harlequin.com

Printed in U.S.A.

Be strong and take heart,
all you who hope in the Lord.
—*Psalms* 31:24

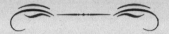

To Dad.

Semper Fi.

You have always been a hero
and I'm proud to call you my dad.

Acknowledgments

I would like to thank the wonderful community
of readers who hang out with me on my
Facebook page. Your presence, support,
encouragement, prayers and interaction mean
so much. I absolutely love the story feedback
you give. You make writing fun!

Thanks also to Elizabeth Mazer, editor
extraordinaire. You are brilliant and talented
and I feel so blessed to be working with you.
Thank you for giving life to Sully and Olivia
through story.

As always, to my family for allowing me
to do this and for cheering me on.

Thank you, Father God,
for knowing what we need even more
than we do. You always come through.

Chapter One

Please don't let this be what I think it is...

"Sully, can you speak?" Even as Olivia Abbott asked her boss the question, his drooping mouth confirmed what her gut already knew. Thankfully she'd learned stroke symptoms this week in EMT class.

"Call 9-1-1!" she directed Patrice, her roommate and a fellow server at Sully's Diner.

"What's wrong with him?" Sully's assistant cook, Darin, carefully helped Olivia lower Sully to the floor beside the food prep counter.

Naem, pulling double duty as server and dishwasher since Perry hadn't shown for his shift again, skidded around the corner. Naem, normally a perpetual grinner, gasped when he saw Sully on the floor. Due to the diner's open floor plan, customers began to notice the activity in the kitchen.

"I think he's having a stroke," Olivia whispered low enough that Sully couldn't hear.

Darin leaped up and, upon entering the adjacent seating area, yelled for help clearing space. After calling 9-1-1 Patrice calmed customers, many of whom jumped in to help Darin move tables and chairs for the first responders. Sizzling sounded as Naem scraped burning food off hot grills.

Please help the ambulance hurry, Olivia prayed as Sully's breathing grew more labored. An EMT student working her way through school by waitressing at the Eagle Point eatery part-time, she suddenly realized that knowing too much automatically gave fear an advantage over her faith.

Sully had an epic reputation for being grumpy but he was the only decent father figure she'd had in her life. He couldn't die on her. Just couldn't.

"Help will be here soon, Sully. I promise."

With his head in her lap, Olivia could see frustration and confusion on his face, and white whiskers he'd missed while shaving. He was meticulous about employees' hair being groomed—he'd obviously not been feeling well this morning. Come to think of it, he'd looked pale and fatigued at the employee Valentine's Day party this past weekend. He'd probably been too stubborn to say something.

Sirens whined in the distance, coming closer. Olivia murmured soothing words to Sully. She was thankful that he'd finally given in to her pestering about having a relationship with God. He had not only started attending her church two months ago, but he'd given his life to the Lord. She hoped he wouldn't need that Heavenly ticket yet.

Patrice, teary-eyed, her lips trembling, knelt next to Olivia and rested her hands over Sully's and Olivia's. "We need to notify his son, Jack. The contact information is probably in Sully's cell phone. I'll take care of calling if you want."

"Yes, please." Olivia knew about Sully's only offspring, Jack Sullenberger, a career Air Force man in Afghanistan whom she'd seen pictures of and heard stories about but never met. She knew Sully missed his boy.

Please, Sully. Hold on and you'll get to see the son you're so proud of.

Patrice retrieved Sully's phone from his office and made the promised call. No answer. She texted. Many moments later Patrice hurried back from Sully's office, phone in hand. "Jack texted back. Said they're going to try to get him on the first flight home."

Tears of relief pricked Olivia's eyes and joy welled as she recalled Sully's mile-wide smiles as he told story after story of Jack—it had assured them of Sully's soft side. Jack the bubbly baby. Jack the toddler, into everything. Jack the mischievous lad. Jack the thoughtful teen. Jack the lady-killer young man. Jack the accomplished military leader.

"Jack should be on his way home soon," Olivia reassured Sully, hoping to help him hold on. She saw a glimmer in Sully's eyes with that. So she scrambled for something else to say about Jack. "You think he's as handsome in person as he is in Sully's pictures, Patrice?"

Patrice caught on to what Olivia was doing. "I know he is. I grew up across the street from him. The girls on my cheerleading squad used to fight over who got to come push-mow our lawn just to glimpse him shooting hoops shirtless. By all accounts he's even better looking now. He had looks and personality. Sweet as could be. Stayed out of trouble and tried to keep the rest of us out of it, too. A true hero, even back then."

Sully's breathing settled, so their chatter about Jack soothed him. Having seen Sully's photos of the striking man, Olivia knew Patrice wasn't exaggerating.

Sully's unsteady gaze traveled urgently to the kitchen, where Naem was keeping everything going on his own, then back to Olivia and Patrice. Olivia knew he was fretting about customers, business and keeping it all afloat.

"Don't worry about anything except getting better, Sully. We got this," Olivia assured.

"Yeah," Patrice added. "Jack worked this place in high school. He'll help us out again."

The look on Sully's face would have been comical if he weren't in the throes of a life-threatening emergency. "We're sure you're gonna be fine, Sully, but someone's gotta help run this kitchen while you're holed up in that hospital. Besides, I hear Jack can flip a mean burger."

Sully relaxed and became less agitated. The EMTs arrived and administered oxygen and meds. Olivia soaked in every nuance of everything they said and did for future reference. She had always been drawn to the excitement of emergencies and trauma care. But it was a whole different experience when the victim was someone she knew.

She needed to find someone to cover the rest of her shift so she could go with Sully to the hospital. Without her, they'd have to close the diner, and that would mean vital revenue lost. She'd be able to sit with Sully tomorrow before her clinical EMT intern shift at Eagle Point Trauma Center, but she needed to be with Sully now, too.

Once on the sidewalk in February's blistering cold wind, the EMTs closed the ambulance doors just as it began to rain. Olivia's silver stud bracelet jangled as Patrice squeezed Olivia's hand. "I know how close you two are, Olivia. Go with Sully. Me, Darin and Naem will keep things running here."

Olivia's tears joined the rain splatters on the sidewalk soaking her rock-and-roll-style boots, but she didn't care. "Are you sure?" Olivia asked.

"Positive. I'll get Jack your number so you can keep him updated, if that's all right?"

"That would be fine. Thank you." She hugged her friend, grabbed her bag from inside the diner and bolted to her clunker. She flipped her wipers on high but the blades barely sluiced the rain off her windows. She pulled out after the ambulance and found the *thwip-thwap* of her wipers calming. Until the ambulance sped up. She did her best to safely keep up until they switched to full lights and sirens one block later. Her chest tightened, making Olivia wish she had her asthma inhaler.

As tears spilled down her cheeks, she knew that Sully's life was in *grave* danger, and that she might never see the light of life in his eyes again.

Dear Jesus, please have mercy on those of us who still need him here.

He didn't need this.

Jack Sullenberger searched the trauma center corridors for room 127. He'd just gotten the latest text from one of Dad's employees—a lady named Olivia—who'd graciously kept him informed over the past thirty hours of traveling.

Thankfully he'd been able to leave Afghanistan the day he'd learned of Dad's stroke. Despite that, it had still taken more than a day to get home. Thirty sleepless, agonizing hours filled with more worry and fear than he'd ever felt in his life, despite serving four back-to-back tours as a Security Forces officer and combat medic in some of the most dangerous war zones in the world.

Whoever this Olivia lady was, he was going to hug her when he saw her, to thank her for staying by Dad's side, talking Jack through medical updates and relaying his decisions to doctors. Eagle Point had no hospital, but the new Eagle Point Trauma Center had an extended-stay wing for situations such as Dad's where the patient was over the initial danger but not stable enough yet to transfer.

Jack rounded a corner and almost plowed into a nurse who stepped aside and motioned him into room 127. The mysterious phone woman—Olivia—had already prepared him for the fact that his dad was still unable to speak. As an Air Force medic, he'd known what the symptoms meant.

Jack parted the curtain and stepped into the room to find a short, pixie-haired waif staring at his dad as if he'd shatter if she blinked. She looked more like she belonged on the cover of a punk-rock magazine than beside a hospital bedside. The scene shocked him so much he froze in place and frowned while his mind tried to work out who she was and why she was here. His jet-lagged brain struggled to process the incongruity between her edgy appearance and her deeply empathetic eyes.

And then she looked up.

Jack's breath hitched. *Pretty* would be an understatement. Stunning? Close, but still not strong enough. Shimmery sapphire eyes shone starkly against alabaster skin, spiky-cropped raven hair and—Jack leaned in to get a better look under subdued light—*purple* lipstick? What kind of person walked into an emergency hospital with intentionally cyanotic-looking lips?

This could not be the soft-spoken Olivia.

Then again, her presence at his father's side suggested otherwise.

Okay, so maybe he wouldn't hug her after all. She looked not so approachable with her nose and ears riddled with piercings, bold makeup, chains for a necklace and a tattoo snaking up the side of her neck. Not to mention her off-limits body language and untrusting eyes as they zeroed in on him approaching the bed. Her rocker-chick look sat at serious odds with the sweet voice that had literally kept him sane and calm on the phone during the last thirty hours.

Her slight smile slid into a frown, prompting Jack to shake off his dismay and find his manners.

"Olivia?" Maybe this wasn't her.

The tiny smile swept one side of her mouth up as she nodded briefly before gazing back at the bed. Distress entered her eyes. He knew the feeling and dreaded facing the hard sight cradled within her eyes.

He'd put the inevitable off long enough. Resisting reality never made it go away. Reluctantly, he forced his gaze off the floor and brought it slowly to the bed.

Dad.

Jack swallowed hard as he approached the frail-looking man engulfed by a huge, flimsy hospital gown. Jack reached through the side rail, took his dad's hand and squeezed. Emotion clogged his throat and an invisible grenade detonated inside his chest. He swallowed but the lump in his throat refused to move. "Dad, I'm—" was all he could manage before his throat clogged again. He was what? Sorry he hadn't been here? Sorry he might be too late? Sorry for deploying for another tour? His father looked so weak, so frail, *so close to death.*

"Sully, Jack's here," Olivia finished for him. Maybe she picked up on Jack's fear because her face softened measurably, then her tense mouth molded into a smile. Wary of giving trust, Jack felt his muscles tighten with the typical guardedness he'd had to develop while working in a war zone amid enemies who sometimes posed as friends. Not wanting to be rude, Jack forced a mannerly smile but it felt thin and strained.

Nonetheless, the chill in her eyes thawed by several degrees as she said, "The doctor says since he got here so fast he'll likely make a full recovery with help from physical, speech and occupational therapy."

The tank sitting on Jack's chest eased off a bit, allowing his voice to come back. "That's good." Relief was an understatement for the way her words made him feel, delivered in the same velvet voice that had kept him calm from one continent to another all the way here.

"Dad, all the guys in my unit said to hurry and get well soon or they're gonna come kick your caboose." He rubbed his dad's hand, longing with all his heart to feel a squeeze back.

He knew that even though Sully slept under medical sedation and stroke aftereffects, he'd likely still be able to hear, since hearing was the last sense to go. Olivia seemed to know that, too. Actually, based on their phone conversations, Jack assumed she'd had medical training of some sort.

He caught and held her gaze. "Thank you, miss, for everything. Most of all, for recognizing what was happening, relaying it to doctors and for getting him help so fast."

She blushed. "Thanks, but it was a team effort." Her shy motions and soft demeanor juxtaposed with her spiky sense of fashion. Upon deeper observation, her intelligent eyes projected a strong will and an expression daring anyone to try and cross it.

She wore a black T-shirt overlaid with a gothic cross in gray graphics. White low-rise jeans sported a black patent leather belt with silver studs. Big triangle earrings and combat-style boots completed her ensemble. Somehow, it worked for her.

And surprised him with its appeal.

She must've noticed his assessment of her because her eyebrows drew down in a scowl. Not the usual female reaction, for sure.

He found her response refreshing, but he was irritated by his own intrigue, especially since he didn't know or therefore trust her true motives for being here. He courteously moved his perusal from the mysterious and mesmerizing creature and shifted his gaze to the drip rate of his dad's intravenous solution and scanned numbers on the machines, glad to see stable vital signs despite Dad's horrible pale color.

"They think he had an undiagnosed heartbeat irregularity." Her brows knit. "I'm not far enough into EMT school to know which kind, but they seemed to think it would be easy to treat."

Jack nodded, deeply appreciative of the information. He'd explain heart rhythms to her in a less intense moment. For now, he needed time with his dad, preferably alone. He needed to say some things and didn't want an audience. His apology was going to be hard enough without a stranger hearing him acknowledge his mistakes in not being here and for being a medic yet not realizing Dad was ill. They video chatted almost nightly. He should've noticed something was wrong. He peered at Olivia but she hadn't budged. In fact she didn't seem the slightest bit inclined to leave.

"I'm sure you have things to do, Miss… I didn't catch your last name?"

"Abbott, and I have nothing more important to do."

Jack shifted to capture her gaze but she seemed even more determined to avoid his eyes. "Thanks, ma'am, but I've got this. You may go now."

Her dark eyebrows slid into a sharp V and her lips pursed. "I'm fine right here, thanks."

Jack had never felt more territorial and annoyed in his life. He was a longtime military leader accustomed to people following his orders without hesitation.

How could this waif of a waitress not get that he wanted her to leave?

She wasn't family. She had no right to be here. Why'd she think she did? It irritated Jack to no end.

As if sensing Jack's thoughts, Olivia narrowed her eyes in a challenge that said if he wanted her gone, he was going to have to physically carry her out.

He was tempted.

Releasing Dad's hand, he marched around the bed. "It wasn't a suggestion, Miss Abbott. I'd like time with my dad. Alone."

She scowled at first, but slowly the tenseness left her shoulders as she studied his face. Then she nodded. She grabbed her gunmetal-gray purse, studded down the sides, leaned over, brushed a gentle hand along his dad's face and said, "Sully, I'll be back tomorrow. Jack will hold vigil until then." Then she slipped out of the room avoiding Jack's gaze.

"I'm walking Miss Abbott out, Dad. Be right back," Jack said, following her.

Once in the hallway, she turned to face him. "I realize this is the first time you've seen your father in person in a while. You're entitled to want time alone with him. I was out of line."

He studied her face like a war map. "Yet you still seem angry about having to leave."

She started to say something then bit her tongue. "He needs someone there. It's your place, not mine. So go back in." She paused to peer back into his dad's room.

A look that Jack could only describe as terror flashed across her face before calm funneled back into her expression. Then she turned without another word and strode away. Jack realized that she was scared to leave his dad. He considered calling her back but then came to his senses. This was a family matter.

This regret was his reckoning. He should have spent time with his dad while he had the chance. But the fact that Sully survived this stroke meant Jack was looking his second chance right in the face. No one was going to take that from him.

Suspicions surfaced as to why Olivia didn't want to leave him alone with Sully. Malevolent ones. Who was she anyway? He didn't know her or her integrity. His dad tended to be too trusting. Jack had never abused his hard-won authority but Miss Abbott, her initial stubbornness, spike-tipped tongue and his twenty total minutes of sleep in three days were driving him to the edge of reason. But hopefully this power struggle between them was a temporary glitch caused by stress and mutual concern for Sully, and would resolve when he stabilized.

A mobile phone chirped from the windowsill. Jack rushed to silence it since his dad was sleeping soundly rather than fitfully now. Upon further inspection, Jack realized this was his dad's new phone. The caller ID said Eagle Point Bank. Jack stepped outside and called them back, introducing himself as Sully's son, explaining that Dad was in intensive care and that Jack had power of attorney.

What he heard next made Jack want to hurl what little food he'd had.

"You're sure about this?" Jack asked the bank officer who'd just explained how deep in debt the diner was, and how many foreclosure warnings the bank had already sent to Sully.

"I'm sorry, Jack. We're sure. I may be able to get an

extension before foreclosure proceedings begin, considering Sully's precarious health. But I can't guarantee it. Especially in light of how much grace has already been extended, and how many subsequent notifications and then demand letters our loan default officer has sent over the past year."

"I understand. Just, yeah, see what you can do. Any kind of extension will help. I'll go over the books and figure out what happened."

Last he'd known, Dad had a cushion financially. What happened? How long had the diner been facing money trouble? Dad had probably kept his financial woes hidden from Jack, not wanting to worry him while he was off at war. His jaw clenched.

"I'll do everything I can," the bank contact stated. "Sully's Diner is a city icon. We'd hate to see it disappear."

Jack would hate it, too—Sully's Diner had been in the family for three generations. "I appreciate the additional grace. Thanks." He hung up and clamped a hand on the nape of his neck. He needed to stay with Dad but also needed to go to the diner and start scouring the books.

"Major General Sullenberger?"

Jack turned. A doctor who looked about Jack's age—early thirties—approached with a smile and extended a hand. "I'm Dr. McLaren. I was here when your dad was brought here to EPTC. His last listed family doctor retired. I'm seeing him as a courtesy while he recovers. At least until we can transfer him to the stroke rehab wing at Refuge Memorial, one town over."

"Nice to meet you. I'm thankful a trauma center was recently built here. Otherwise…" Jack didn't need to finish. The sober look on the doctor's face completed his thoughts. Had the trauma center not been close and Dad's

employees not gotten him help when they did, Sully may
not be here. "I'm ashamed to admit I wasn't aware of his
doctor retiring, and I'm not sure why he never got a new
doctor. Maybe if I'd known, this could have been prevented." Guilt riddled Jack.

"It's hard to say." The doctor wrote something down
on a pad and handed the page to Jack. "Here are some
local doctors. One's a military veteran, like your dad.
He'll need to have a primary care physician to follow up
with as he progresses through all the poststroke therapy."

Jack studied the list of four names and numbers. "I'll
make some calls and also see to it that he takes better
care of himself." As he said it, he knew that would be
difficult if he returned overseas.

Jack had some hard decisions ahead.

"You look beat. You should go home for the night
and sleep. We'll call if anything changes. Right now,
he's stable and needs rest and quiet more than anything.
As do you."

Jack peered down the hall toward his dad's door. He
didn't want to leave but knew the doctor was probably
right on all counts. He nodded in resignation. "Okay."

"Meanwhile, we have an Olivia Abbott listed as your
dad's emergency contact. Is that correct?"

What? Why Olivia? For sure, Jack needed to figure out
why this Abbott woman was so entrenched in his dad's
life and business. "If you'd please change that to me, I'd
appreciate it. I'm also his medical and legal power of attorney." Jack gave the doctor his contact information. "I'll
be staying at his apartment above the diner."

"Got it." An overhead page called the doctor to another area of Eagle Point Trauma Center—EPTC. He
gave Jack's information to the nursing staff and jogged
toward the stairs.

Jack returned to his dad's hospital room to spend a few more moments with him before heading out. As he sat there, Jack wrestled with scenarios and hard questions, and a particular pixie face floated into his weary, wary mind.

Olivia Abbott, her soft voice at such odds with her edgy look, her tender affection toward his dad equally at odds with her ink- and stud-abraded skin. She was *totally* not his usual type.

And maybe that was *exactly* why he struggled to take his thoughts off her. But at this point, it was too early to tell whether he owed her an apology or a closer look in terms of her background and her motives. The doctor was obviously right. He needed rest. Sleep would rid him of the jumble of unexpected thoughts, fears, feelings, accusations and attraction ricocheting around his tired mind. Right now, his guardedness trumped anything else he might be feeling for Olivia Abbott. And he aimed to keep it that way.

Chapter Two

"So much for first impressions."

Three days after Jack's arrival, Olivia spread a vinyl tablecloth over the pinewood breakfast nook of the apartment she shared with Patrice. It was one of two units situated above the diner. The fact that work was literally downstairs was a huge blessing of convenience to Olivia—it made it easier for her to put in as many diner hours as she could between studying and classes and her intern shift at EPTC. Especially in light of the learning disability she kept hidden from others.

"Jack's all bark and no bite. Don't worry."

"I don't know, Patrice. He seems to get angrier by the day. He was in Perry's face again this morning."

Granted, she felt that was warranted, because Perry had cursed so loudly at the sinks, customers heard his rant in the dining room. She guessed Jack was also justified in telling Perry to text on his own time. However, threatening to run Perry's phone through the dishwasher seemed a little extreme. Of course, that was after he'd already asked him multiple times to put his phone away and get to work unless on break.

"I realize he's undoubtedly worried about his dad,"

Olivia said. But there was more she wasn't telling Patrice. Jack was fretting over the diner, too. Quite by accident, she'd caught bits of conversations he'd had with bankers and loan officers. She'd eventually moved the condiment filling station away from the office to keep from overhearing what should be a private business matter.

She wondered how much Sully knew of it. She'd appreciated Jack asking the bank people not to tell Sully how bad things were yet, so soon after his stroke. That the Sullenbergers were a well-respected family undoubtedly helped.

Patrice pulled out a small paintbrush. "He's not himself, that's for sure."

"Sully or Jack?" Olivia teased, hoping to lift the melancholy cloud from Patrice's eyes.

Patrice smiled. "Both." She set a craft caddy on the tablecloth and grew serious. "It's been so hard working in the diner without Sully there. Memories of him are everywhere."

"True." Emotions were high and Jack had been one to avoid. It was a little tough since he was staying across the hall in Sully's apartment. Not that he was there much. He'd either been at the hospital or downstairs at the diner holed up in Sully's office going over financial records. This afternoon, he'd emerged like a loaded tank looking for targets. He even seethed around Patrice, his pal since childhood. Not that Patrice seemed to notice—she was entrenched in another argument with her boyfriend, on par for their volatile relationship. "Still," Olivia added, "he has one of the most intimidating personas I've ever encountered." She'd tried her best to steer clear the past two shifts. That seemed to suit Jack just fine because he appeared to go out of his way to avoid her, too.

"The military must've changed him a lot. On the other

hand, he was always one to stand up for others and act with honor and integrity."

Olivia opened two packages of paints, one forest-colored and one in glittery jewel tones as Patrice set poster board on the tablecloth. "In fact, I can't believe Jack made you leave the hospital that first night."

"I can. He was bossy as all get-out." Olivia held the glossy white cardstock in place while Patrice painted Get Well Soon, Sully onto the homemade card in beautiful flowing calligraphy.

They were making Sully a huge card for diner patrons and employees to sign. Patrice was a fantastic artist. If she'd ditch her oppressive boyfriend, her dreams of a graphic design career would surely come true.

Patrice dotted red glittery firework shapes along the card's edge. "Take into account Jack was probably scared out of his wits and sleep-deprived from his cross-continental flight."

Recalling the look on Jack's face when he saw the shape his dad was in kicked Olivia's conscience into gear. "You're right. It must have been a shock."

Patrice nodded and capped the red paint lid before opening the blue to create glittery sapphire stars. They'd chosen the colors in honor of Sully's patriotic nature. His entire diner decor consisted of veteran and war memorabilia spanning decades, all the way up to the present.

Patrice switched to silver and painted swirly scrolls next to the stars. "I hope this cheers Sully up and shows him he's well loved despite his being a grump."

Olivia snickered. "At least we know where Jack got it from."

Patrice giggled. Then frowned as a text notification came through her phone. "Uh-oh. Speaking of Jack... he's calling a mandatory emergency employee meeting."

Olivia's pulse sped up. She had a busy week making up the clinical hours she'd missed while sitting with Sully. She also had classwork to catch up on and a huge medical research paper due soon. She couldn't possibly fit one more thing into her week. "When?"

Patrice nibbled her thumbnail. "Not sure yet. He's giving the time in a forthcoming text."

"I wonder what the meeting's about." Olivia's pulse ramped up even more. Were things at Sully's bad enough financially that they were all going to be laid off, or worse, let go? "Patrice, I overheard Jack talking to the bank. I hope he's not going to close the diner."

Patrice blinked in surprise. "I can't imagine. He practically grew up there. His childhood wasn't easy. He spent more time at the diner with his dad than at home with his mom."

It wasn't Olivia's business, but she couldn't help but ponder why. She'd had a rough childhood herself and felt instant compassion for others with tough childhoods.

Patrice sighed as she completed the gorgeous card. "Jack was a good kid. A model child. Very compliant. And Sully was a model parent. He removed Jack from a volatile situation." Patrice shook her head and seemed to snap out of her musings. "But I suppose that's all Jack's story to tell."

Not that he would ever, in a trillion years, trust Olivia enough to feel comfortable sharing personal information. Everything about Jack Sullenberger screamed unscalable walls and immovable rules.

Why was it that something in her wanted to breach and break them all?

Olivia tried to imagine Sully's struggle on behalf of his son, which led to thoughts of Jack as a boy and how hard that must've been. She didn't know Jack's story and may never.

However, she could relate to living in a troubled home. But unlike Sully, her dad had never fought for her, and knowledge of that always put a hard lump in Olivia's throat.

Precisely why Olivia promised herself not to pursue relationships, but rather to secure a college degree and a career with which she could support herself for life. Not dating was easy, since she was so wary of men. The degree, however, was an uphill climb due to her dyslexia. But she refused to let it—or anything—stop her.

She was thankful Sully worked around her school and clinic hours to allow her adequate time to study. He was one of few people who knew about Olivia's learning disability. Patrice, Darin and Naem were the others, but that was it. If anyone else found out—especially Jack—she'd be mortified.

She'd squirmed under the scrutiny of his gorgeous, gunmetal grays assessing her appearance at the hospital. His obvious shock at her style dinged her dignity and dented the armor of her hard-sought self-esteem. He was so strong and good-looking, his opinion mattered to Olivia more than it should. She didn't like having to work so hard to not care what he thought of her.

"Naem told me this morning before the breakfast rush that Jack told him and Darin that he's officially here on an extended military leave."

"Until when?"

"I don't know." Patrice's phone bleeped with another notification. Olivia blew on the card's paint to get it to dry faster as Patrice read her text. "Oh, wow. He called the mandatory emergency staff meeting for tomorrow morning at seven."

"Seven?" Olivia chirped. That would cut into her best sleep time. She worked the day shift at the diner, did evening EMT classes alternating every other day with clinical at EPTC and spent half the night studying until around two in the morning. She then slept until seven thirty, which was just enough time to roll out of bed, shower and dress before starting breakfast prep at the diner at eight. She'd been able to survive on so little sleep simply because she'd known she wouldn't have to pull this schedule forever. Now Jack wanted to shake things up? Great.

He'd already upset her by sending her away from Sully. It still smarted that he'd made her leave and didn't seem inclined to let her visit anytime soon. But that wedge was Jack's doing and Olivia was struggling to have a right heart about it.

A band of tension tightened across Olivia's shoulders, making it hard to breathe. She was already stretched to the max. Jack's plans were bound to increase stress and decrease rest. How would she ever manage to comprehend past her dyslexia while running on fumes for sleep?

Olivia liked things at the diner just as they were. Sully was great about working around her school hours. She doubted, considering everything he was contending with, that Jack had the patience or presence of mind to do the same.

"You okay, Liv? You don't look so good."

Olivia didn't have the energy to correct Patrice about the nickname she hated. "Feeling a little light-headed and wheezy."

Patrice reached for Olivia's asthma inhaler and popped the cap off. She rarely had a stress-induced attack, but this felt like one of those times. Desperately short of breath now, Olivia placed the oval in her mouth and pumped the prime twice, inhaling deeply each time. Once she could breathe unobstructedly and speak again, instead of clawing her collar away from her neck in air-hunger panic, she thanked Patrice, who asked what triggered her attack.

"Change. I don't like the sound of it. Not at all." Never had. And for good reason. In Olivia's experience, change equaled something awful. It always meant moving from a bad situation to a worse one.

"Miss Abbott, you're late." Jack watched Olivia's cheeks flush as she rushed around the table to the empty seat at the diner employee meeting the next morning.

Her face awash in a strong emotion he couldn't decipher, he stared her down. Her scowl loosened and she promptly sat. "My apologies."

"No explanation?"

She swallowed. Bit her tongue. Then she said, "None that you'd understand." Her scowl tried its best to return but she fought it.

Wait. What did she mean he wouldn't understand?

"That means?"

Now her scowl did return. She peered at the clock. "Please, if you don't mind, we all have other places to be."

He guessed she was right. And to credit her defense, he hadn't given them much notice. He relented on ripping on her for being fifteen minutes late to what he'd hoped would only be a half hour meeting. He moved to stand at the head of the table in the staff break room and studied the group of a dozen or so employees. He met each gaze, finding himself irritated when Olivia intentionally looked away. As angry and flustered as she appeared, he half expected her to get up and walk out. Then he noticed something else. Dark, sunken eyes and drawn features. As if she hadn't slept well, or maybe not at all.

He tore his gaze, and his compassion, away from her and faced the group. After all, if he got soft, they'd continue to run all over his dad...*if* he was ever able to take over again.

Until then, Jack would handle it. "Some things are going to change around here, now that I'm in charge."

Jack watched Olivia stiffen at his mention of change. A pallor flushed the scorch out of her cheeks from when she'd sprinted in, windblown and breathless.

He knew the feeling. This was a big turning point for him, too—choosing to stay for an extended period of time in the town he'd avoided for so long.

"First order of business is—"

"Like, what kind of changes?" Perry, the dishwasher, interrupted Jack for the third time since he'd started the meeting.

Tired of the disrespect, Jack placed his palms flat on the table and leaned in, face-to-face with the young man. "For starters, you get fired if you pull a no-show again without calling in."

Perry's mouth dropped open. "Dude, that's harsh."

"Asking that you call if you're not planning on showing up is not an unreasonable request. Furthermore, if you're late more than three times in a pay period, you're fired." Jack didn't give Perry a chance to launch another argument before pulling out the schedule.

Olivia visibly tensed. He peered at her, making sure she didn't have something to say before he continued. "Miss Abbott? Did you have something to add?"

Her eyes scanned the schedule, then lowered. "No, sir."

"Yet your body language states that you do."

Hands formerly folded in her lap flew up past her shoulders. "Fine, I just know how Sully would want things done.

He doesn't believe in fixing something that isn't broken and with the exception of a few glitches, the schedule works fine the way it is."

Jack shook his head. "That may be the case, but we have lost too much revenue."

She looked as though she didn't know what that had to do with the schedule, but she'd find out soon enough.

Jack actually admired her pluck. Unlike Perry, she didn't present as rude. Just strong in her conviction to stand up to him to defend what she thought his dad would want. A measure of admiration rose up in him but he quelled it in order to keep the meeting on track and be able to get them out of here. Their time was as valuable as his.

Several exchanges later, it became apparent to Jack that Olivia was not one to back down easily from something she believed in. Change was apparently not something she believed in.

However, she did apparently believe in trying his grace and patience to the max.

Tension bundled in the back of his neck and spread to his shoulders.

As though sensing his thoughts, she lifted her chin. "I'm only trying to help."

Jack wasn't so sure. She seemed bent on opposing him at every turn. Regardless, in light of the time crunch, he found himself increasingly irritated that she wasn't simply taking orders. At least Perry had simmered down to a quiet sulk.

Hopefully Olivia's spunkiness wouldn't turn her into a troublemaker or drag things out here. Especially considering a fourth of them were working the morning shift today. Soon.

Choosing, for time's sake, not to engage Olivia's stubbornness, Jack spread the schedule out and clicked its identical image on his video presentation. "First order of business is cost control. Starting today, I want syrup and sugar shakers only half filled on tables. Ketchup and mustard will only be placed on tables when customers ask. We'll also use—"

Olivia's hand shot up.

Jack paused. "Yes, Miss Abbott?"

"I'm wondering how that will cut costs."

"I was getting to that," he said with more edge than he'd intended. "If the containers are full, customers will inadvertently use more." It had worked in the service. He hoped customers would catch on. "We'll also use cloth napkins instead of paper."

Olivia raised her hand again. Jack fought irritation at the intrusion. "Yes?"

"Cloth napkins will need to be washed and dried. That will use electricity. Electricity costs money. Plus the water needed to wash the towels. And detergent. That costs money, too."

"I'm well aware of the costs, Miss Abbott. I'm installing new efficient washers and dryers. If I've estimated correctly, cloth is far more cost effective. Especially since Eagle Point customers love to smuggle handfuls of our paper napkins out in their pockets and purses."

She nibbled her lip but didn't argue. Yet the expression on her face clearly said *and you don't think they'll smuggle cloth napkins out, too?* Cloth would be less of a temptation. Most customers would feel bad taking them home. Hopefully.

And just because he was irritated, Jack added, "Only fill the salt and pepper shakers halfway, as well. I'm also going to crack down on tardiness and missing food items. That means you will fill out inventory sheets each time you use something up. No more taking boxes of meat home," he directed to Perry, whom he knew had taken a box for a barbecue and beer bash at his house and hadn't paid for it. "Or any other food and supplies, for that matter. Taking something that's not rightfully yours is considered theft and is grounds for termination. Do I make myself clear?"

"Can we buy cases of stuff if you have enough?" Naem asked.

"If we have plenty of it in stock and you note the transaction on inventory sheets, yes."

Naem nodded. Perry sank lower into a slouch, bad attitude wafting off him like steam.

"Next item on the agenda is hours of operation. I have no idea why Dad did this but it's not prudent to delay opening a restaurant until nine in the morning. That's a lot of lost revenue from potential early eater breakfast patrons."

His voice seemed to have obliterated all the air in the room because Olivia's face paled. Naem, Darin and Patrice slid Olivia glances that told him there was definitely a story behind why his dad had decided to open the diner later and close it earlier. That story had to do with Olivia.

Other employees, waitstaff plus another assistant cook from the opposite shift, began to notice the shift in the atmosphere because they darted glances between Olivia and her day-shift crewmates. No matter. He couldn't be derailed or they'd lose the diner. And, in turn, everyone sitting here would be unemployed. He couldn't let that happen.

Furthermore, saving the business that meant so much to his father was Jack's chance to make it up to him for not being around.

Dad's narrowed hours of operation had been a bad

move. That initial bank call on Dad's phone at EPTC had nearly put Jack in the stroke wing beside his father. Jack hated taking drastic measures, but the business would go under if he didn't. He couldn't let Dad's future fade without a fight. That meant staying open during ideal meal hours. The diner's precarious financial state and Dad's health had made huge impacts on Jack and cemented his decision to stay in town and take over running the place.

"Effective immediately, we will open at six a.m. and close at nine p.m. on weekdays, seven a.m. on weekends with closing time at ten p.m. That means I need the morning crew to be here an hour before opening and the evening crew will need to stick around an hour or so after closing to get things ready for the next day."

Several eyes shot to Olivia. She kept her face down. Jack looked at her hands, tightly clutching her bag strap. She was squeezing the fiber out of it. Obviously, by the sympathetic looks rallying around her, the new hours would be a hardship on her. But Jack was not about to let his family's legacy die because one employee had issues with inconvenient hours. He felt firm about it and wise in his decision.

So why, then, did mercy needle his conscience over Olivia?

"Guys, I know this is a lot to take in. But it makes the most sense. Okay?"

Everyone, including Olivia, nodded. But she never looked up. Jack would pull her aside later and privately ask her why she was upset about the hours. He didn't intend to stress her out. He just wanted to save the family diner and secure Dad's future. Especially if Sully ended up unable to return to work.

That would throw Jack's life into a tailspin. He'd always envisioned himself serving decades in the military before retiring. At this point he still planned on returning to duty once Dad and the diner got back on their feet. He'd wanted to reach twenty years of service. But fate clearly had other ideas. He wished Olivia knew he understood how she felt. Sully's stroke had sent several lives into chaos. They needed to band together and do what it took to get through this.

After going over other items of business, Jack concluded the meeting and bought his employees breakfast out of his own pocket. It was the least he could do. None of this was their fault.

Rather than eat her meal, Olivia slid the tray toward Darin and sprang out of her chair. Jack watched her friends' concerned, crestfallen expressions as Olivia rushed out the door. Jack tossed Darin the diner keys, called, "Take charge until I return," and sprinted out the door after her, not even sure why, and convinced he was making a mistake.

Yet something compelled him to do it anyhow.

She barely made it to the end of the block before he slowed his pursuit in order not to startle her. She was obviously lost in thought and oblivious to his approach.

"Miss Abbott?"

Her steps stuttered but didn't stop.

"Please wait. I just need a moment of your time."

She paused but didn't turn around. Her arm came up to swipe across her face—she was crying.

He stepped close enough to rest a hand on her shoulder. "Olivia."

She stiffened at his use of her first name. It had surprised him, too.

"What?" she said in defeated tones, her back still to him.

He came around to face her. "Talk to me."

She huffed. "There's no need. I'm fine."

"Considering you shot out of the break room like a rodeo bull from a stall, I don't believe that. Help me understand."

She shook her head, clearly exasperated. "There is nothing to understand. I told you, I'm *fine*." The involuntary tremor of her eyelid informed him otherwise.

But she obviously didn't feel comfortable being vulnerable. He thought back over the meeting and her reactions at certain points, then mapped together possible scenarios.

"Miss Abbott, what part of the new schedule is a hardship on you? Maybe I can work around the issue."

That was absolutely not what Olivia expected Jack to say.

The strain in his voice told her that working around her schedule was going to cause a problem. She already knew that but hadn't wanted to face up to it. The diner was not in a good place financially. The bank wouldn't care what reason they gave. If they didn't get their money, they'd foreclose.

"The new hours will not be a problem," she hedged. Even though her weary mind strained toward being open with Jack, she could not.

It would be selfish to expect the entire restaurant, and by extension the community, Sully and her friends, to arrange their most precious resource of time around her, and she could not bring herself to do it. Not after everything Sully had done for her.

"It's a prudent decision given the diner's debt," she added.

"That's not your problem, though."

"And my scheduling conflicts are not yours. So trust me to work it out and I'll back off on inserting my titanium opinions at future employee meetings. Provided I still have a job."

Jack's lip twitched, as if he were about to crack a smile, probably because she'd so accurately described herself.

"I haven't fired anyone. *Yet*."

"I get the feeling Perry's the period on the end of that statement."

Jack's jaw clenched. "He's irresponsible, insubordinate, rebellious and inconsiderate. Not to mention far from dependable. I have gone above and beyond to teach and warn him."

True. But that Jack would actually fire him rankled, even though she respected his rationale. The day crew stuck together like glue.

"You resent me."

Was that a question or a statement?

Yes, she resented him a little. He wasn't Sully.

Yet maybe that was exactly why Perry got away with so much. Sully had let stuff slide.

Apparently a lot of stuff.

Jack shifted and checked his watch. She hated that they were still clashing, but there was something about him that set off the worst and weakest aspects of her character. Not to mention that the last thing she wanted was for such a strong man to see her fragile and upset.

She raised her chin to try to be more tough and convincing.

He examined her in that probing way of his.

"If you need special consideration—"

"I do not." She'd just have to suck it up, nap when she could, study harder and pray her guts out for God to help her understand the things she read in her brick-thick medical books. Once she learned something, she had impeccable recall, but it was the initial challenge of getting the data in, and her brain's ability to comprehend it, that was the struggle. Even her dyslexia could be contended with. The comprehension problem that was aggravated by lack of sleep? Not so much.

Olivia sat at a crossroads, literally. As Jack waited patiently, peering at cars whizzing by, she knew she had a choice to make. And it wasn't going to be easy. In fact, it was probably the hardest thing she'd ever have to do—concede defeat and come clean.

She had to succeed in her goals, and if that meant eventually breaking down and sharing her disability with her new boss, she'd do it in order to keep herself from failing the EMT program. But she wouldn't tell him until absolutely necessary. He had enough to worry about without her neediness. The last thing she wanted to be was a burden.

He gestured to a sidewalk bench between two Bradford pear trees. "Please, sit a moment."

With gritted teeth, she said, "I'd rather not. Please forgive my emotional outburst and abrupt exodus from the meeting, Mr. Sullenberger. Now, really, I must be going."

Mainly because the earnest care in his eyes was starting to get to her.

"Please, call me Jack. May I call you Olivia?" A corner of his mouth curled into a smirk-lined smile, acknowledging that he hadn't exactly waited for her permission on that front.

The joking tone and flash of amusement in his eyes surprised her. She hadn't figured him as the type.

She nodded stiffly, keeping her chin down lest she lose her nerve for what she needed to say next. Then she looked up at Jack and said the last words in the world she wanted to say. "The new schedule won't be a problem. It needs to happen. I know that. It's fine."

Jack stared at her. He leaned back, rubbing his thumb and forefinger along his lower lip, studying her in that calculating way of his. Shook his head. Leaned forward, steepled his hands and released a breath before raking all ten fingers through his buzz, which looked more light brown than dark blond, as it had in Sully's photos. "You are one stubborn broad."

She burst out laughing because he'd muttered it mostly to himself. And because it was true.

His eyes lit at her laughter and then he laughed, too. For a moment she felt frozen in time. He was drop-dead gorgeous, even when he scowled like his father, but with his finely chiseled face all loose in laughter like that, good gravy he was finer than fine.

Where were they? Oh, yes, her stubbornness.

"I'm not trying to be difficult or stubborn. I just don't know any other way to be."

"You've had it rough. No need to deny it. You've had to fight for everything you have."

She peered at him, shock waves rolling through her. "How did you know that?" Did his dad say something?

"Intuition. And because I haven't always had it easy, either. In fact—"

"In fact it's mostly been hard," she finished for him.

"Exactly. So, will you share with me what the trouble is?"

She nibbled her lip, wondering if she could trust him. Would he use the knowledge as power over her? Maybe. He was a hothead. The next time he got mad, he might revert to meanness and spite, just like her dad always did.

No. She couldn't risk it.

"No, Jack, I'm sorry, I can't."

"I guess I have to accept that. For now. But, believe me, I'm not happy about it."

She could tell that his equally stubborn brain was already churning out ideas about how to get around her resistance.

Speaking of resistance, she needed to shore up some of her own. The way his muscles rippled under that button-down shirt and the attention his intense facial expressions brought to his firm jaw and striking features stole every ounce of concentration from her brain.

She couldn't be attracted to him. That infatuation would fade soon.

It had to. Trust was too dangerous a journey to embark on. She was not only instinctively wary of trusting, but also unsure of Jack. Sure, he was handsome and she was admittedly attracted. Even if he returned the attraction, she couldn't let herself acknowledge it. Dwelling on insurgent thoughts of opening up to him as anything beyond employee and employer would be stupid. Trust issues aside, he couldn't treat her differently just because she had special needs he didn't know about yet and hopefully never would. Olivia didn't want special treatment. Her coworkers and work friends didn't deserve that.

The diner crew was close-knit. At least, her shift of workers. She'd pull Jack into the fray of diner friendship if he let her. But she wouldn't entertain ideas about ever being anything to him other than his employee.

She was also a pity case his dad had taken under his wing. He'd taught her everything she knew about waitressing, studying and running a business.

But as far as Jack Sullenberger knew, she was just Olivia, nothing special.

The fact that Jack was looking at her with an expression that suggested he thought the exact opposite was something she'd be better off ignoring.

Chapter Three

"You have three months on the nose, Jack," the loan officer said through the diner office phone the next morning. Jack rubbed tired eyes with his fist, first one then the other. Then he covered another yawn.

He had burned the midnight oil in order to finish going over the books. He'd finished at 5:00 a.m., expecting to find answers regarding the enormous deficit, but ending up with more questions. He'd been going over the books a second time when the loan officer called.

"I don't need much to live on," Jack said. "I'll have most of my checks sent directly to the bank to be applied to the diner deficit until I track down these missing funds." It would cut into his savings but saving the diner would be worth it.

"Another thing to consider is that perhaps your dad's faculties were failing and he got confused keeping records."

"Yet his inventory records and every other record stayed impeccable? Not likely. Things don't add up."

But the more likely scenario wasn't any more appealing to Jack than the possibility that his dad had made accounting errors.

Had someone been stealing from the till? Taking funds from somewhere? Too much money was missing and unaccounted for—this wasn't a simple record-keeping mistake.

He ended the call with a bad feeling.

From this point onward, Jack would trust no one. Not even Patrice. Frankie, that creep boyfriend of hers was a bad influence. Jack knew his type—spoiled, entitled and cunning as a conman. Bad morals corrupted good character. Without exception. No telling if he'd had access to the register. Jack didn't like him hanging around the diner.

Darin's face appeared in the office doorway. "Jack, sorry to interrupt you, man, but I'm getting slammed out here." Sweat dotted Darin's forehead. He mopped it with a paper towel.

Then Jack realized his entire apron was soaked. And sudsy. Which could only mean one thing.

"Perry isn't here yet?"

Darin averted his eyes. Then returned to face Jack with honesty. "No. He hasn't called, either."

Jack rose to help wash dishes. He studied the clock. Perry was thirty minutes late so far. He shook his head, irritated at the lack of work ethic. He sighed, knowing he was in a precarious spot.

Perry was late.

But Olivia had been late, too. Only by about ten minutes, but still.

She'd rushed in much the same way she'd entered the meeting yesterday—tardy, flustered and fatigued. If he disciplined Perry, he'd have to discipline her, too.

He grabbed the dish towel from Darin. "I'll handle the dishes. You go man the grill."

Darin nodded and Jack headed to the sinks. He passed

Olivia on the way. She stood at the condiment prep table filling containers.

Filling containers *all the way up*. Sugar. Syrup. Salt. Pepper. Ketchup. Mustard.

Then she placed every single one of them, filled to overflowing despite his request not to, on her rolling cart and took them toward the dining area.

He stared in disbelief as she started plunking down mustard and ketchup containers on every table.

Just as he'd asked her not to do.

He counted to ten before he blew his stack.

Not only did he likely have a thief on the loose—which meant he was going to have to be diligent in watching everyone like a hawk every minute until evidence presented itself—he had to contend with gross disrespect of his authority.

Naem rounded the corner whistling. He was in a perpetually good mood—it was hard to stay in a bad mood around him. Jack's lightened mood dampened when Olivia passed by looking irritated.

Actually, it didn't seem as though she saw them. Her back to them, she darted into the supply closet across the hall from the office. Seconds later, she groaned. "Mister Tough-Guy-With-All-His-Rules. Couldn't leave well enough alone. Ugh!"

Who and what was the addled woman talking about?

Naem stopped in front of him. And grinned. "You look about to blow a gasket, boss. What's she done now?"

Jack shook his head. Then he heard another groan coming from the supply closet.

"You heard her call you Mister Tough-Guy-With-All-The-Rules or what?"

Jack almost laughed at that. "She actually said that about *me*?"

Naem flipped a stack of cloth napkins over his arm. "Hey, if the combat boot fits…"

Olivia jerked her apron string tight as she exited the closet and started shoving more salt and pepper shakers on the wheeled cart to distribute to tables.

He realized on closer inspection that she actually looked more frazzled and drained than irritated.

Empathy filtered in until he noticed something else. Every shaker was full.

He fought another surge of anger as he realized she'd defied him again by filling every single one of those containers to the hilt, as well. He watched as she doubled the efforts of her rebellion by tromping over and setting mustard on every table.

Mister Tough-Guy-With-Rules?

If that was the case and he was stuck in his way with rules, Miss Olivia Abbott seemed bulldog determined to break or at least bend them all.

Olivia remembered halfway through her table-to-table setup that she wasn't supposed to be putting the containers on tables unless customers asked for them. She groaned for the gazillionth time today and started taking them back off. One hour of sleep was not nearly enough. She felt disoriented and memory challenged.

By now, Jack had marched to the kitchen in that clenched-jaw way of his, stopping only to help Darin by heating up the extra grills since they'd been busier than anyone had anticipated at breakfast. Jack headed to the back leveling a firm look her way. If the pans banging around the sink now were any indication, Jack had seen her mistake with the tables. *Uh-oh.*

Only she doubted he'd believe it *was* a mistake.

"I forgot," she said to Patrice who raised The Mom Look eyebrows at her.

"Did you also forget he said he didn't want the syrup filled up all the way?"

Ack! She'd forgotten that, too. Her brain was foggy from fatigue. Admittedly, Jack's ideas made her bristle. "That's dumb. That means more work for the next person on shift. He's trying to save money. I get that. But filling the dispensers only half full will not make customers use half as much. It will just make us have to work twice as much to keep things refilled."

"You may be right, and he'll eventually figure it out…" Patrice bit her lip but Olivia knew the rest without Patrice having to spell it out.

"Fine. Whether I agree with him or not, it's what he requested and I need to honor his wishes." Olivia shrugged, feeling bombarded from all directions. He wouldn't understand that she'd barely slept a wink because she'd been too stubborn to be straight with him yesterday when he'd probed her with questions on the sidewalk after the employee meeting.

Just knowing she'd had to get up earlier had set off her insomnia like a bull running through her bedroom. Her thoughts had been a dizzying array of chaos and she could not shut them down. She'd started counting sheep and ended with visions of them turning on her with loaded shotguns.

The longer she'd lain there trying to fall asleep, the sooner morning came, and with every hour closer to the time her alarm was set for, her anxiety grew into a frenzy over having one less hour to sleep. She'd finally given up, gotten up and studied, hoping that would help. It hadn't.

Olivia slipped outside and went for a walk, hoping the cool air would help her feel more alert. On the way back in, she passed Jack's truck—a Ford, of course. It reminded her that Sully had often spoken of frequent Ford-versus-Chevy sparring between he and Jack. Olivia sided with Sully on that one. Chevy rocked! She fought the urge to write a note on his truck. She'd promised Sully to razz Jack about his love of Fords. But somehow Jack didn't seem the joking type now that she'd met him in person.

Adding to her stress was the pressing reminder that, at some point, after sneaking downstairs overnight to study in her favorite corner booth, she realized she'd studied the wrong chapter and therefore put herself in danger of not passing her test later today.

Maybe she needed to just be honest with Jack about her limitations.

Would it make a difference? She went to the supply room to run it by Patrice.

She, of all people, knew how much Olivia hated to be treated differently or given special attention. Yet did she have too much pride to admit that she may need extra help?

Also, telling Jack would mean running the risk of him hiring someone else, which neither of them could afford.

The hair on Olivia's neck stood at attention—she sensed Jack's overpowering presence before she saw him.

"Miss Abbott, I need to see you in my office."

Jack stalked back to the office and Olivia stood amid the patriotic diner decor feeling as if she were in the middle of one of the wars the wall images depicted. She fought fear and hyperventilation. She liked it soooo much better when he called her Olivia. Addressing her so formally meant she was in trouble.

Patrice started to head back toward the office looking intent to be a verbal buffer but Olivia stopped her. "It's sweet of you to want to defend me but I need to face the music myself."

Patrice paused. "You sure?"

Olivia nodded. She didn't want to put her friend in the line of fire. "Jack looks too angry to bend even if you try to talk him out of whatever he plans to say."

Patrice nibbled her lip. "Or do."

"Oh, Patrice, what if he fires me? I should have re-membered what he said in the meeting."

"Go, before he gets madder."

Olivia made the trek feeling as if she was marching to a chopping block. First, he cut her off from seeing Sully. And now…he may boot her out of her only source of in-come. Not that she didn't deserve the latter.

She stepped inside Sully's office. Jack was sitting at the desk with his head bowed over a spreadsheet of some sort. He didn't even bother looking up before saying, "Please close the door and sit down."

She obeyed instantly—as she should have all along this morning—as she tried to figure out how to explain what had happened. He'd never believe her, after she'd questioned his money-saving judgment yesterday, that her actions today hadn't been defiant or deliberate.

Maybe she'd assumed wrongly that he was like Sully, often forgiving to a fault. Something about Jack's silence told her that he was not the same way. She gulped. Hard. Felt a fidget coming on but was too terrified to move.

Jack stopped writing on the sheet and stood so calmly, she shivered.

"I'm sorry," she blurted. "Please let me keep my job."

If she lost her job, she couldn't pay for school and she'd fail at life.

He blinked in surprise, then quickly covered it by scowling as he waved her comment off. Still, the little telling gesture made her think there may be some Sully in Jack after all. "I'm not going to fire you, Olivia. But I am going to ask for your cooperation in doing what I say so things can run smoothly for all of us."

"I know. When you ask me to do something, you expect me to do it."

"That lecture is not why I called you in here and if you were getting proper sleep, mistakes like overfilling the syrup and sugar wouldn't be happening."

She stood. "How do you know I'm not getting proper sleep?"

He gestured toward her apron. "It's on seam-side out." Next he pointed to her name tag. "And, last I heard, you aren't Oliver."

She looked down and clenched her eyes shut. Groaned. Felt like giggling.

In her defense, Olivia and Oliver were very close in spelling. Except Oliver was the maintenance guy.

She didn't refute Jack's statement about the lack of sleep. She did, however, rapidly right her apron.

"The full containers are not my biggest concern. New habits take time."

She stiffened. "Then what?"

Had he discovered her disability? She felt equal parts relief and trepidation. Truly, his response depended on his mercy.

Or lack thereof. She honestly didn't know him well enough to guess to which side he'd lean.

He shuffled papers before meeting her gaze again. "It seems you have very strong opinions as to how this diner should run."

Yes. She did. But only because of Sully and his leeway and how much he'd grown to depend on her with his health taking a nosedive and his refusal to see a doctor.

She opted for humor and blinked innocently. "What on earth would make you think that?"

A quick flash of dimples bracketing his smile told her she'd caught him off guard. But he quickly righted his rigid posture and drill-sergeant demeanor. "If you were a shift manager, what would you suggest I do about Perry's on-the-job drug use?"

"Uhhh… I don't know what you—"

"Don't lie to me. I won't keep people I can't trust."

Her shoulders sank. "Jack, I really didn't know."

Jack tossed a pencil on the desk. It rolled off and bounced on the floor.

Clearly, he didn't believe her.

Wait, wait, wait. Why would he mention her in conjunction with management?

Olivia felt bronchial spasms that usually preceded a stress-driven asthma attack. Sully didn't believe in putting one employee above another. Surely Jack wasn't scouting out which of them to stick at the bottom and top of a chain of command, was he? That could breed resentment and compromise the bond they all shared.

No matter. A more pressing issue blared between them.

She swallowed. "What drug use are you talking about?"

"He pops pills."

"He has a lot of allergies."

Jack smirked. "Yeah, to staying sober and straight. I noticed his pupils were dilated. I asked to see the bottle. He refused. That threw up a red flag. I'm a medic—I've had pharmacology classes. I suspect the pills he's taking are someone else's prescription."

She sat. "Narcotics?"

"Yes. I can't have employees impaired on the job. It's dangerous for the employee, for their coworkers, for customers and it's an insurance liability. Not to mention a lawsuit waiting to happen. If he shows up today, I'm doing a drug test. If he refuses, I'm letting him go. In fact, to be fair, everyone gets a drug test today. It's the law and Dad has never performed one to my knowledge."

She blinked. Was he questioning each of them about Perry? She'd seen him call Naem, Darin and Patrice in earlier, individually. While she was glad Jack wasn't singling her out, it bothered her that he didn't believe the best about her and the others. Either he had trust issues, too, or something had happened to make him suspect something amiss.

Olivia thought back to what he'd said about not wanting his employees impaired. Yet, isn't that what she was, this sleep deprived?

She was no safer to have around than Perry, in a sense.

Jack studied her all the more intently, which made her wonder if his impairment concerns were why she'd been called in last. Maybe he'd questioned them about her, too.

She *had* to get more sleep. Period. But how?

The clacking of plates and platters and an increasing din wafted through the wood door. Things were starting to sound chaotic out in the dining area, which meant the floodgates had opened.

"Can I go? I really need to help Patrice and Naem. Obviously you were right about patrons eating breakfast early."

In fact, many things had been running more smoothly. If she told him, would he think she was just sucking up? *Was* she?

"One more question. Who all has access to the registers here?"

"Pretty much all of us. We all help each other in a pinch."

He apparently didn't like that answer because his jaw clenched rhythmically. "Employees only?"

"Yes." Why would he ask that? Had someone taken money? They'd been really lax about counting registers at shift change, and Sully operated almost solely on an honor system. She just assumed everyone was as honest as she was.

The thought that someone would steal from Sully upped her ire in a big way.

Patrice could be heard calling out for Darin to bring her more menus, which meant she and Naem were probably dealing with a full dining room. Olivia darted glances toward the door, wanting to go help her crew out of breakfast-rush chaos. Plus, Darin was undoubtedly slammed, too, and could use Jack's help on the grills and other food prep.

Jack rose. "Go on back to work, Liv."

She jerked. "Why did you call me that?"

Jack angled his head. "Dad told me to."

"How? He's not speaking." She stood. Sat. Stood. "Is he?"

"He started writing with his strong hand on a special tablet last night. Have you not been to see him?"

She scowled. "I assumed you didn't want me to."

"I never said that. I just needed time alone with him that first evening."

"So you don't have a problem with me visiting him?"

"Not as of now." He studied her in a way that made Olivia wonder if he suspected her of unethical behavior, as well. "I'll say it one more time. I can't keep people I can't trust. Do I make myself clear?"

Olivia nodded but a terrible fist clenched her gut. Bottom line, Jack did not trust her. Why? What did he think she'd done, or what did he think her capable of?

She couldn't stand the thought of being let go. That would stress Sully out. And keep her from paying for school and make her ineligible for the EPTC internship scholarship. And maybe force her to live with one of her parents, a very unhealthy atmosphere. She just couldn't. He *had* to believe her.

Olivia wasn't sure why his opinion mattered so much, just that it did. What he thought of her was important to her, even if she didn't want it to be.

"You can trust me, Jack."

He leaned back in his chair and folded his arms across his well-developed chest. "We'll see."

After nonstop customers from the start of her shift to the end, Olivia's feet were aching. She'd expected to get to use her breaks for studying the right chapter but ended up not even having time to eat. She went to class and bombed her test despite cramming the hour before.

Her schedule was too packed. Something had to give. She came home feeling defeated and praying for sleep. Still, it eluded her and she hadn't been able to comprehend a single thing in her book. Her dyslexia was functioning at an all-time high. She needed help. Period.

The next morning, she at least made it to the diner on time. Just in time to hear Jack say his trademark, "Get your boots back to work," to Darin and Naem, who were swatting each other with wet dish towels.

When she walked to the back and glimpsed Jack yanking Perry's time card out of his slot, she realized that Perry had not shown up yesterday. She eyed the clock. Patrice, just now arriving, peered at the clock as well. "Perry's late again," Olivia whispered.

"That's his problem. I've got issues of my own."

"Fighting with Frankie again?"

Patrice lifted her sleeves. Fingerlike red marks covered her upper arms.

"He did that?" Again!

Patrice nodded, tears filling her eyes. "He shook me so hard I bit my tongue."

"I'm so sorry. I keep telling you, you need to get away from him. Why won't you listen?"

"I know. But I can't." Patrice shrugged with the shoulders of someone already defeated.

Olivia wanted to talk sense into her, to ensure her safety, but Patrice looked too distressed right now to listen. That talk would have to wait. For now, out of sensitivity, Olivia sent Patrice the kindest smile she could and tried to think of worthwhile words to say.

Naem interrupted them. "Trouble's brewing. Jack is at the computer cutting Perry's check."

"Since today's not payday, that's not a good sign," Olivia said.

"No. Maybe if we have a talk with Perry and he promises to do better, Jack will relent."

She nibbled her lip, recalling the conversation about impairment and possible drugs. "Naem, I'm not sure that's the best decision."

Naem looked at her funny. "Hey, we all stick together. All us little people." Naem eyed her, then Jack. "What were you doing in his office, anyhow?"

Olivia realized the potential for distrust and division. "He had questions about the diner." Olivia answered carefully. "Probably the same questions he asked you, Darin and Patrice."

Naem nodded. "He said he needs to speak to me again today. Darin's in there now. Maybe we should all compare notes."

"Maybe."

As she and Naem donned aprons, washed hands and

tucked pens behind their ears, Darin emerged from Jack's office. Wordlessly he headed straight for the grills.

Perry was nowhere to be found. She eyed the clock. He was twenty minutes late.

Jack helped Darin prepare bacon, then took over washing dishes. After customers started piling in upon the diner opening, a surprise to Olivia because she hadn't thought they would continue to, day after day, Perry rolled in looking hungover and unkempt.

He only got four steps in before Jack pointed to the door.

Perry stopped, lowering his spit bottle. Gross. How could anyone chew tobacco in a restaurant? Not to mention it was a major health-code violation and one even Sully wouldn't tolerate.

"What?" Perry blinked at Jack, who looked more livid by the second.

Perry on the other hand, looked as stoned as he probably was.

"No." Jack barreled around the corner to stand in Perry's way. "There's the door. Walk back through it. You're done here." He handed Perry his final check.

"You're firing me 'cause I'm only an hour late? What up, dude?"

"Out. Now. Or I'll call the police."

As mad as Jack looked, Olivia mentally advised Perry to do what Jack said. The anger in Jack's eyes told her that calling the police on Perry was the most humane of two choices. Getting tossed out on his ear by Jack was probably the less appealing of the two.

As Jack walked Perry out, he said, "You need to get professional help."

Perry sneered and muttered something to Jack that

probably would have earned him a fist in the face from a less-controlled man.

"Oh my. I cannot believe he actually fired him," Patrice whispered later to Olivia as they tucked order pads into the next shift's aprons. Everyone had been walking on eggshells since the incident.

You mess up once, I warn you. You mess up twice, you're done. That's what he'd said when they'd all gaped at him after he escorted Perry out. Zero tolerance. Since then Jack had not said another word. To anyone.

"I know. To Jack's credit, Perry pushed him over the line. He was warned," Olivia said.

"Yeah. Multiple times. Still."

Nothing else needed to be said. Olivia knew one thing. She wasn't about to cross Jack. He was nothing like his dad. Sully might yell a lot, but he was all bark and no bite. Maybe even passive to a fault when it came to setting boundaries with employees. Jack, on the other hand? He was all bite. Little to no mercy seemed his mantra.

Other than that Fords were the only car built tough and worth having. Olivia smiled fondly remembering Sully telling her of their Chevy-versus-Ford sparring. Though Sully had made her promise to give Jack a hard time about Ford once she met him in person, so far, she hadn't had the nerve.

"Of course he could have been using Perry as an example." Patrice shrugged.

"To show his power you mean?" Olivia hoped not. But it bothered her that Jack didn't even try to find out Perry's background. Or, if he had, she wasn't aware of it.

"I don't know. Maybe. That doesn't seem like the Jack I remember, but maybe the military and war changed him." Patrice didn't have to finish the rest.

Changed him. And not for the better.

Just as Olivia thought. Change was, at this point in her life, her absolute worst enemy, and right now Jack Sullenberger was captaining that particular moving ship.

Chapter Four

Jack knew his firing of Perry had rattled the tight-knit day-shift crew yesterday. They were still subdued and somber today. Everyone, even Olivia, had shown up for work extraordinarily early and no one was goofing off or joking around.

He hated to be the bad guy, but Dad had been too passive in dealing with insubordination and misconduct. Behavior like Perry's could end up being bad for business.

He'd done the right thing by setting a precedent.

Yet he felt the gap widening between himself and his employees over it.

"Hey, Jack, the appliance delivery company is on the line." Patrice held up the cordless phone as lunch customers walked through the jingling door.

"Patch them through." When his office phone beeped, he punched a button. "Jack Sullenberger speaking."

"Yes, sir. Eagle Point Appliances. How are you today?" a chipper female voice asked.

Dismal. "Fine. What's up?"

"Well, aren't we Mr. No Nonsense again today," the clerk teased in cooing tones.

Jack rubbed his temple, willing away the oncoming

headache as she chattered on. She sounded like the same gal who'd flirted relentlessly with him when he'd gone in to order the new washer and dryer for the diner yesterday, after his evening visit with Dad.

Yes, loneliness resided that felt like a canyon was widening inside his chest more every year. But he'd seen enough emotional and psychological pain between his parents in his growing-up years to last a lifetime—and to sufficiently keep him away from any marriage-minded woman.

As far as Jack was concerned, he was married to the military.

"Listen," he interrupted her. "We're kinda busy here. Could you get to the point?"

Silence. He heard a brief huff, then, "With the impending threat of bad winter weather, we'd like to deliver the washer and dryer early," she said in a more professional tone, yet laced with enough saccharine and sarcasm to let him know she felt rebuffed and wasn't happy about it. "Today, if possible, since the storm's supposed to get worse tomorrow and terrible the day after."

"That's fine."

"One issue is that all of our delivery drivers are out and we may need manpower for lifting."

"Not a problem. I'll be here and we've got strong guys to help."

After writing the delivery time on the calendar, Jack hung up when the clerk attempted to turn the conversation personal again. He didn't have time for this nonsense.

His dad's rickety office chair squealed as Jack swiveled to peer at the diner's ancient computer monitor. Yesterday, the loan officer had mentioned sending digital reminders. Up until then, Jack hadn't realized Dad had a diner email account. "What's the password to the diner's email address?" Jack called to Olivia, who was stacking server ware across the hall on the stainless steel shelving. "And why are you putting that stuff there?"

Olivia started to furrow her brows then recovered quickly. "'I don't remember,' and this is where Sully wants the plates stacked." She turned to get a tray of cups.

He stalked to the doorway. "If you don't know the password, then who does?"

"Your father...and the password *is*, 'I don't remember.'"

"'I don't remember.' That's literally the password?"

"Yes. Because that's the only password your father could remember. He uses it for everything."

"Then everything he has will be hacked." Jack sighed over the security breach. "Did Dad give anyone else here the password?"

"I don't know, but I don't think so."

Good and bad. She'd have access to financial records, but it also meant Dad trusted her more than the others. Why? He intended to do some digging.

"Perhaps you should turn up the heat in here," she suggested, glancing at the customers huddled inside the door. "They're complaining that it's too cold."

While Jack was inclined to argue with Olivia, she was probably right. "A few degrees and no more," he said. "We have to get the electric bill down."

He lifted his wrist to check his watch. He'd need to pick up some diner supplies before the ice storm hit. He couldn't really go right now because someone needed to be in charge while he was gone. Jack needed to establish an employee chain of command in the diner. He'd start observing more closely to see which employee everyone looked to in each of the two shifts.

Since Naem was taking care of customers, Jack handed

Olivia a Rolodex and notebook. "Here. Before we get too busy, I want you to come up with a different password for all of Dad's accounts. Write them down and I'll keep the info in the safe from now on." Jack worried Sully trusted Olivia too much. This test would show him if she deserved it. He surprised himself by hoping so.

She looked at the items skeptically and slid into the office seat he indicated.

Thirty minutes later, Jack asked, "How close are you to being done?" It didn't seem like it should be taking her this long to create a few dozen passwords.

"Maybe halfway," she answered in a voice that sounded as strained as she looked. She practically had her nose to the Rolodex, so close he wondered if she needed glasses.

"Only halfway?" he said, surprised. Then instantly wished he could take his words back.

Crestfallen, she slid the Rolodex back into its holder. Her shoulders slumped more than a moment ago. She looked toward the door as if she wanted to flee. He hadn't meant to hurt her feelings, embarrass her or make her feel bad.

"It's fine. I'll finish it. Go ahead," he said, motioning her back to help Naem since more customers had come in.

"I'm sorry," she mumbled as she stood and slowly closed the notebook. Her cheeks were tinged pink and she averted her eyes as Jack studied her.

Had the task taken longer because she had a vision issue? Or something else entirely?

"Olivia, is there a problem I should know about? Your eyes, maybe?"

Her sharp intake of breath told him he was close and that surprised her. "No," she said quickly.

If she didn't tell him, he couldn't help her.

After Olivia left, Jack checked the radar and turned up the weather alert radio's volume. Snow flurries had begun and were expected to morph into a full-fledged winter storm that was expected to worsen this evening and last all weekend.

Snow wouldn't be bad, but if it turned to sleet or ice, as predicted, that would be bad for business and another financial hit. If people couldn't drive or get out, they couldn't eat out.

He sighed and scrubbed a hand down his face. What else could go wrong?

A knock sounded on his door. Olivia peered in with a strained face and slid a pen behind her ear. "Jack, one of the grills isn't heating properly."

He stifled a groan and rose. He expected her to scurry out of his way but as he approached the door, she didn't move.

Nearly face-to-face, he paused. "Yes?"

"I—I just wanted to talk with you about something personal."

Her eyes darted to the worn floor, then bounced up to his then away. She looked embarrassed or ashamed. His heart softened toward her.

"Yo, Jack! Might wanna come see this," Darin called. He sounded panicked—a rarity.

Olivia stepped out of the way. "But obviously it can wait."

Jack reluctantly nodded and went to figure out what was wrong with one of the two grills and considered praying that the problem would be an easy fix. A sudden putrid electrical burning smell sent his headache through the roof. No telling what his blood pressure was up to right now.

"Shut it down," Jack commanded, moving toward the

breaker that powered the diner's only industrial-sized coffeemaker. Wispy smoke and snapping sparks flew from the cord near the outlet.

Jack jerked it out of the blackening wall and turned to get the fire extinguisher—and ran into it coming toward him, thanks to Olivia. *Quick thinking*, he thought, but for some reason he couldn't say the words. Why did he have such trouble giving praise and compliments yet it was so easy for him to give orders?

He guessed he'd figured that if he warmed up to the employees, or at least let his soft side show this early, they'd try to walk all over him and disrespect his rules. In his line of work, troops lived by rules, died by not following rules.

Better to make them think he was a heartless hardball so he could maintain authority and order. That was the only way to get things running in the black in time to save Bully's.

After dealing with the shorted-out coffeemaker, Jack instructed the staff to make coffee with the smaller pots for now, then went to check on Darin. On his way, he caught Olivia studying him with an overtly irritated expression. What now?

She quickly recovered and spun to take a tray of food to customers.

Darin's eyebrows rose. "What's that about?" He nodded toward Olivia.

"Who knows?" Jack grinned, remembering Olivia's blush when he caught her openly scowling at him when she thought he wasn't looking. "I was hoping you could tell me."

Darin laughed. "Right. Figuring women's feelings out requires at least a PhD in physics, surgical access to their brains, and an engineering degree, none of which I will ever have."

Jack paused. Something in his tone told him Darin believed that. "Hey, you're more intelligent than you give yourself credit for."

Darin paused in scraping the sizzling grill. "Thanks, but all my life I was told the opposite."

Jack's compassion surged for Darin. He determined to offer encouragement, at least to Darin. He wasn't one to fish for compliments, and in fact, the linebacker-sized, tatted-up guy appeared to cringe at Jack's admonishing words. "I believe in you, man."

As Olivia swept past with a second tray of food, her head whipped around at Jack's words. Surprise was clearly evident in her eyes. In fact, she almost dropped the tray.

Just what did that say about Jack and her poor impression of him?

Better question—why was he concerned about her impression of him at all?

He shoved the thought out of his mind and, as he often did, said sternly to the crew, "Get your boots back to work."

That they smiled and resumed their tasks meant he'd let too much of his soft side show.

He turned and eyed the clock. Olivia was supposed to be on break by now, but he was glad she was helping Naem since folks out shopping in preparation for the winter storm were giving them a surge of business. Still, it probably wouldn't be enough to replace the deficit the storm would bring, or the lack of business the snow would leave in its wake.

"This is not going to be an easy fix," Jack muttered when he finished inspecting the unevenly heating grill. He started walking down the hall to get the toolbox. A few steps later, moisture plopped on Jack's head. His jaw clenched as he paused and peered at the ceiling. Sure enough, water dripped from it.

He had a choice. Fix the grill or fix the ceiling. He couldn't do both at the same time.

He mopped up the mess, put a bucket under the drip temporarily and grabbed the phone book. *Ting-ting-ting-ting.* He gritted his teeth at the sound of water pinging stainless steel.

"Jack, I was going on break, but…is there something I can do first or instead?" Olivia's concerned gaze let him know he needed to hide his stress better.

He was going to tell her no, but the weight of reason kicked in. No sense in not letting her help if she was willing and it could get them past a time crunch. "Can you look up the numbers for roofing companies? Figure out the best one with the most reasonable prices. Ask for references. Have them come take a look." He gestured to the leak. Then he remembered her struggle earlier and wanted to kick himself for asking her to do something that would humiliate her again.

"Your dad uses Eagle Point Eaves and Gutters. It's speed dial 4 on the office phone."

Jack paused. Winced that she knew that and he didn't. "So, I'm guessing if Dad had the roof repair company on speed dial, he's had problems with it leaking before today?"

"Yes, recently it's gotten worse." She nibbled her lip and wrung her hands.

He shook his head. "The health department would have a fit."

"Jack, I hate to say this, but the main grill's not heating at all now," Darin said while flipping patties from the large grill to the smaller one, which may not hold the volume they needed, depending on incoming orders.

Jack went over, shut the main grill off, instructed Darin to use the small one for the time being and then went to get a plastic tub to catch the leaking water. On the way to the supply room, Naem caught him. "There is an angry customer demanding to see you. Something about the sidewalk not being deiced and his wife almost slipping."

Jack sighed. He needed to run to town and get more ice melt. Since when did it sleet here this time of year? Oh, well. He couldn't waste time dwelling on how things were supposed to have been. He needed to focus effort on figuring out how to deal with the unexpected changes, just as he did overseas. "Please call the roofers to come immediately," he directed Patrice. To Olivia he said, "Catch a quick break."

The consternation on her face made him wonder if he'd offended her.

He couldn't worry about that right now. The diner was falling apart around him.

Then he heard them mention Perry and he knew they were thinking what he didn't want to admit. He could have really used another pair of hands today, even if those hands had shown up late.

Jack only let that thought reach the edges of his brain before kicking it back out.

He wouldn't budge on his rules. To do so would cause more damage in the long run.

Naem rushed past with a slightly panicked expression and a bin full of dirty dishes, making Jack realize how low they were on clean supplies. He needed to hire someone to replace Perry as soon as possible. He hadn't had a chance to go through all of the applications from the job ads he'd placed online for local people.

On the way back through, Naem did a double take when he saw the charred wall and coffeemaker. "Dude, what else can go wrong today?" he muttered and shook his head. For the first time ever, Jack saw him without a smile.

"What else can go wrong? Are you serious, Naem? I really wish you hadn't voiced that out loud. If life has taught me anything, it's that things can always get worse."

"Yeah, dude, but they could also always get better, too."

Jack was trying to figure out a nice way to tell Naem to shut up when his cell phone rang.

When he saw that it was EPTC, his pulse spiked.

Olivia watched Jack. His usually steady demeanor had been replaced by short, sharp motions and increasingly agitated expressions. It seemed that, like the snow, his aggravation was cumulative. As he tried to maneuver both the phone and the dish sprayer—which she knew from experience had about a 3000-PSI mind of its own and required two hands no matter who was handling it— water shot onto the floor.

Listening to the caller, Jack paused and pressed the phone closer. His face was ashen. "Are things under control now, though?" he asked the caller while continuing to wrestle with the sprayer.

Olivia clicked her tongue. "Stubborn man is going to electrocute himself." She marched back out of the break room and took the sprayer from his hand, leaving him with his mouth open and his eyebrows furrowed.

She ignored the protest in his expression.

She untwisted the sprayer and aimed it at the dishes,

clearing food off in a few back-and-forth swipes of powered water.

After a moment, color returned to Jack's face. "Okay. Keep me informed of any changes." He hung up then continued to watch Olivia's spray-cleanse technique a moment before shoving his phone in his pocket and holding out his hand. "Gimme that thing."

The urge to laugh probably would have accosted her had she not been worried the phone call was about Sully. Fear prevented her from asking. If there was bad news, Jack would tell her, right?

Right now, he looked only like he couldn't stand to let the sprayer get the best of him. Or perhaps he just didn't want to be shown up by someone half his size. She bit back a grin.

Olivia handed over the nozzle but stayed to watch the debacle. That sprayer had taken her months to master, and she was very mechanically inclined. No way was she going to miss out on seeing Jack try to tame it in thirty seconds.

Three minutes later it became apparent the sprayer wanted to go one way and Jack another. He started muttering angrily under his breath—the sprayer wasn't giving up easily. Jack's sleeves and the front of his shirt were soaked.

The day's stress was beginning to show on him and the rest of the crew. They were starting to snip and snap at each other, which rarely happened. And Jack? He looked beyond overwhelmed. Olivia suddenly felt the inexplicable urge to ease the tension from his eyes.

Maybe she'd made the right choice after all, not telling him about her dyslexia. He didn't need another thing to stress him out. Plus, he'd treat her differently, which she didn't want.

He gritted his teeth while wrestling with the industrial sprayer hose as though it were a huge writhing viper. "What is *wrong* with this stupid thing?"

She smirked at the opportunity to kill two birds with one stone by getting a dig in and maybe making him smile. Mostly though, she just wanted to get a dig in. "Operator error?" she joked.

He glared at her above the wiry, dancing, spouting-sideways hose. "Not funny."

Realizing her joke had backfired and growing more determined to see him smile, Olivia scrambled for another way to make him laugh. She recalled his and Sully's running Ford-versus-Chevy debate.

"Okay, then the only other reasonable explanation is that it was probably made by Ford."

His head whipped up and he blinked at her. His eyes narrowed until he saw her smiling. A flash of humor transformed his face into something exquisite. So much so, it took her aback.

She swiftly turned to get back to work. That wily plan had totally backfired on her. Jack Sullenberger was too cute for her own good when he smiled like that.

Moments later Patrice sidled up next to Olivia, menus in hand. "Did you tell him?"

"No. We got interrupted." She was glad now that she hadn't had a chance to go through with revealing her dyslexia to him. "Besides, I'm having second thoughts. I have a feeling it would just make him more impatient with me." Of course, she could be wrong. She didn't know him well enough yet to be able to tell how he'd react.

"I'm not sure, either, since he doesn't seem like himself. Hasn't since he's been back. Being overseas has definitely changed him. The Jack I used to know would be understanding."

"To his credit, it wasn't fair of me to pretend to be okay reading through Sully's chicken-scratch writing." All the letters jumbled together in the middle of the index cards. "My reading techniques helped some, but not fast enough for Jack's liking." And fatigue had hastened her miscomprehension.

Her pride hadn't let her admit her problem to him.

Patrice gave Olivia a pat on the back and an empathetic smile while glancing toward the back where Jack contended with problems. He was hunkered under the utility sink, now glaring at the drainpipe with a wicked-looking wrench and a ferocious expression.

Lord, how can I help? Do I step in? Or stay out of his way?

Olivia pondered this as she started loading bowls and plates into the dishwasher trays so they wouldn't run out of necessities. It dawned on her that humor was key in managing Jack. When she joked with him, he gave her that incredible smile. It made her want to keep him laughing. Should she? Or would that plan backfire by making her emotionally vulnerable to him in ways she was terrified to be?

Thoughts awhirl, she turned to get clean towels and realized Jack was speaking to someone on the phone again. She grew concerned at the strain in his face as he spoke to what sounded like another doctor.

She tried not to eavesdrop. Hard, since she heard him mention Sully.

It made her wonder again if the previous phone call was in regard to Sully, as well. Panic seized her. She could worry herself into a useless puddle of fear. Or she could pray.

Lord, watch over Sully. Fix whatever's going on. You are trustworthy and in control.

Dishes started, she turned to wash her hands and realized they were out of soap. She went to grab a refill from
the stockroom. Just then Jack let out a sigh and marched
out of the office, nearly plowing into her. She nodded to
his phone. "Is everything okay with your dad?" she asked.

His jaw tensed. "No. Can you come off break early?
I need to run to the trauma center."

Fear tried to grip her but maybe God had provided
a barrier with her prayer because she felt somehow removed from it. Still, if something was wrong with Sully,
she wanted to be there, too.

And, yet, she wasn't family. Furthermore, they were
sinking here at the diner and barely able to keep up with
Jack present, much less without him. No way could she
leave. She swallowed the urge to ask Jack to let her ride
with him. What was wrong with Sully? Jack didn't seem
inclined to tell her anything.

"Olivia," he said in firmer tones. "Can I count on you
to do what I asked?"

Her insides roiling with frustration at the situation,
and fighting a fresh surge of fear over Sully, she forced
calm into her tone. "Yes."

She couldn't be with Sully, but her prayers—and by
extension God's presence—could. She said a prayer for
Jack, too, since today was one disaster after another and
had been all day. Plus, he probably had stress she didn't
know about.

At the door, Jack met an appliance delivery person
armed with a clipboard. Jack checked his phone and let out
a grunt. "Bring it to the back. Naem, come help Darin load
this in. I need to go make nice with the guy whose wife
almost fell. Olivia, make sure their meal is free today."

His crew nodded and dispersed to duty. After checking on the woman who'd nearly slipped and apologizing

to her husband, Jack returned to where the guys had unloaded the washer and dryer.

"I'll need you to sign here in order for the diner to be billed," the delivery driver said to Jack.

Jack's head whipped up. "Did the appliance center clerk not tell you?"

"Tell me what, sir?"

"The washer and dryer are being paid for by me. Not the diner." Jack glanced at his watch. Scribbled a signature onto another form.

"No, sir. She did not pass that along. I'll have to fill out another form in that case."

"I don't have time for that." Jack reached into his wallet and yanked several hundred-dollar bills out and shoved them toward the man. "Here's what I have in cash. Send the forms to me digitally and I'll send the rest of the payment by phone. Do not charge my dad or the diner a cent for these appliances. Got it?"

"Y-yes, sir." The driver put his clipboard under his arm and pulled out a pen. "At least let me write a receipt for the cash—"

Olivia stepped forward. "I'll handle getting the receipt. Go ahead," she motioned to Jack and the door. "Go on." He needed to check on Sully. *She* needed him to check on Sully.

Jack wavered. Peered at the cash, then Olivia, then the delivery driver. His jaw hardened. Did he doubt that they'd be honest about the amount? Olivia's backbone stiffened at the thought.

Why did he automatically believe the worst about her instead of choosing to believe the best first?

With a stern look of warning to them both, Jack rushed out the door, where he set down an A-shaped sign on the walk that said "Caution—slippery." Then he left in his navy blue Ford Ranger with the US flag and eagle decal gleaming patriotically from the back window.

It connected to Olivia's realization that keeping Jack laughing was the key to keeping him low key and happy. So far, the only way she'd been able to do so was with the Ford joke. She decided then and there that Sully's admonishment to torment Jack over his die-hard love of Fords was on the menu and a great, neutral way to keep Jack laughing and lower his stress. Remembering a Ford wall calendar Jack hung in the office, she went in and, snickering in tribute to Sully, wrote FORD=Fix Or Repair Daily on the calendar, then recapped the Sharpie and got back to work. Jack needed to learn how to laugh again.

No wonder Sully had insisted on a Chevy when he'd helped Olivia purchase a car.

She left the office laughing. So perhaps the jokes were good for lessening her stress hormones, too.

Naem updated Patrice and Olivia on his patrons' meal statuses and then told them he'd be back as soon as he could, after getting the ice melt for Jack. He counted the bills, showed them to her, Darin and Patrice, then stuffed them in the outer edge of his wallet. "Money out of his own pocket, I'm assuming," Naem said.

"He also paid for the washer and dryer himself," Olivia confirmed.

Naem, Patrice, Darin and Olivia all shared a glance. "Things must be bad financially," Darin said. "If this place goes under, Sully will be crushed."

"Guys, we can't let that happen," Olivia blurted, emotion welling for Sully. How she missed him and missed his advice, even his surliness. She'd give anything for a lecture right now.

"I agree. We need to figure out how to help," Naem offered.

"Yeah. So let's put our heads together," Patrice said, then all three of them looked to Olivia. "If you have any ideas, we're all ears."

Why did they always look to her? She was probably the least capable of all.

Yet an idea struck.

Olivia approached the delivery guy. "How much is left on the bill after the cash?"

"Seven hundred dollars, ma'am."

"Okay. Can you wait a few minutes for the rest?"

"Yes, ma'am."

She told Patrice to cover her tables, then rushed upstairs to her apartment.

Two months ago, Sully had given her a thousand dollars as a Christmas bonus. She'd put it in her cedar jewelry box to help with books for next semester or for emergencies, as Sully had suggested. She counted out seven hundred plus another seventy dollars for a tip for the driver, for having to put up with Jack Sullenberger's bad mood and untrusting attitude.

She ran back downstairs trying to convince herself she was doing this only for Sully.

It had nothing to do with the growing pool of mercy in her heart for Jack. Nothing at all.

After paying the clerk, she handed him the tip.

"Wow, this is a lot. Thanks, ma'am."

"Sure. One thing… I don't want anyone to know who paid the remainder. Promise me?"

He looked up from writing the receipt. "Okay. But what if Major General Sullenberger asks?" The delivery guy didn't look like he wanted to get on Jack's bad side. Still…

"Tell him it was taken care of anonymously."

She put the paid-in-full-with-cash receipt in Sully's

safe and closed it securely, deciding not to tell anyone she'd paid the bill. That way, no one would feel bad if they were unable to help in the same way.

She'd think of other ways for the crew to help.

She gripped her phone and thought about calling the hospital. She normally could do her schoolwork online but had a mandatory EMT class tonight at the college for a certification that she could not miss. She had a clinical tomorrow evening. She'd just show up at EPTC early and see about Sully. He was like family whether Jack liked it or not.

She couldn't stay away, not knowing what was wrong or what the call was about. It frustrated her that Jack didn't feel inclined to tell her how Sully was doing. Then again, he had no idea how close she'd grown to Sully. How would he react if he knew? Would he be angrier? More suspicious of her? Because she had no idea, she couldn't risk his knowing.

Regardless, she wasn't going to let his silence deter her from being there for Sully.

She just needed to figure out how to do so in a way that kept her off Jack's radar.

When the one o'clock shift change happened, they'd become so inundated with customers, the day-shift crew offered to stay and help the next crew through the crunch. Nevertheless, Olivia went to the time clock and swiped her card.

Naem paused behind her. "What are you doing?"

"Clocking out. But I'm still staying to help. I don't want Sully to have to pay overtime."

Naem pulled his badge and clocked out, as well. Then grinned at Olivia.

"Naem…"

"It's fine. Sully has helped us all out at various times. We owe him this much."

Darin approached. "What's going on?"

Patrice slipped between the two. "We're working an hour or two for free." She swiped her card through, too. "Every little bit helps, right?"

Darin grinned. "I want in on this clandestine clocking out." He sliced his card through, then went back to the grill. Olivia's eyes filled with tears. None of them could really afford to do this, but the truth was, Sully may not be able to afford them *not* doing this.

"God will pay us back, Olivia. Don't look so shaken," Naem told her.

She looked at the precious soul. "You're always so positive. Even when things get bad."

"Because things eventually get better," he said. Then whistled as he got back to work.

Though clocking out at one, Darin, Naem and Patrice stayed and worked until three. They'd all agreed to do it to help Sully and the diner. Yet Olivia felt nervous about Jack's response.

Hopefully Jack would let Patrice or Olivia do payroll and he'd never know. For the first time in her life, Olivia was truly grateful she had a problem processing letters but not numbers.

Now, if she could just stop this rabid worrying over Jack's eventual reaction, she'd be better off and more able to focus. She only had thirty minutes to study.

But she couldn't shake the nagging sense that because Jack was so conditioned by the military to rigidly follow rules, he'd be livid if he knew they'd worked off the clock.

Therefore, she needed to try and keep him from knowing for as long as possible. Right?

Jack came back later and went straight to his office.

Two minutes later, he poked his head into the break room and held up his calendar with a stern but funny arch to his brow. "Are you the miscreant who desecrated my Ford calendar like this?"

Olivia pressed her lips together but the pressure became too much. She burst out laughing. Jack shook his head and flopped the calendar overtop her head. "Payday's coming, Olivia. You just started a war you can't win."

While Jack did his best to act irritated, Olivia loved the laughter in his eyes.

When she went to leave for the day, Patrice was snickering in front of her locker.

Olivia peered around Patrice's shoulder to find her locker completely covered in Ford bumper stickers. To the point where her locker was glued shut from them. "Really, Jack? Is that all you've got?" she hollered out the door and began ripping stickers off in order to get to her purse.

Once in, she gasped. "He did not!" She yanked her favorite hoodie out, gasping at the message he'd written in bold blue ink above her Girls Have More Fun logo. He'd written FORD in similar letters so that her favorite hoodie now stated Ford Girls Have More Fun.

She slammed her locker shut and pounded on his office door, behind which she could hear him snickering. "This had better not be permanent marker, Jack."

A deeper snicker met her threat. She had to admit preferring the pranking side of Jack over the surly, aloof side. She grinned on her way out the door saying, "Sully, you're not even here and you know how to fix things." A bittersweet wind swept over her. Olivia was all too happy to step in and razz Jack until Sully got well enough to take the razzing right back over. *Please, Lord? In Your mercy, heal and restore him. Sully's the only dad I feel like I've ever had.*

When she reached her car, she realized a note was blowing in the wind under her wiper. Thinking it was a sales or solicitation flyer, she pulled it out only to realize Jack had struck again. The note said, "To the contrary, Olivia, FORD=Found Often Rescuing Duramaxes."

She giggled despite herself. Then an uncomfortable sensation seeped into her as she wondered how much of her family history Sully had shared with Jack—her mom was a mechanic who specialized in Duramax engines.

The thought of Jack knowing her past and hard upbringing made Olivia feel a little too vulnerable for comfort.

She'd come to Eagle Point to get away from her childhood, not to be reminded of it.

This thing with Jack was getting more complicated by the minute…which was the last thing she needed.

Chapter Five

$\sim\!\!\!\!\!\sim$

Jack set aside the new diner policies-and-procedures manual that he'd been working on when a knock sounded at Sully's hospital room door the next evening. He rose to greet the visitor and to let the person know to be quiet since Dad was finally resting after he'd had an allergic reaction to a medication.

He opened the door to see Olivia standing there. She was in a deep purple hospital scrub uniform and startled upon seeing him.

"I heard he had a setback. I just came to check on him," she said with slight trepidation.

Jack stepped back and waved her in, whispering, "He's stable now but resting. We should keep our voices down."

She nodded and peered around him to where Sully lay in the bed. Jack turned back to study Olivia as she watched his dad sleep. Worry lines creased her forehead. If she was faking how much she cared, she was a great actress. "Have a seat," he offered, indicating the recliner.

She shook her head. "That's okay. I need to get started soon. I'm on my clinical rotation shift here at EPTC."

He nodded but concern riddled him for her.

Olivia looked weary, her features were becoming more

drained by the day. He hadn't been at the diner much since coming to the hospital yesterday. "You look tired. How late did you stay at the diner after I left?"

She shifted her weight from one foot to the other. "I clocked out around one." She averted her eyes and Jack got the distinct impression she was keeping something from him.

"That's not what I asked. How late did you stay?"

"Until three."

His jaw clenched.

"I don't mind."

"That's not the point." It was a liability for her to work off the clock. Why had she? He really didn't know what to think of it. He took in her attire, and her EPTC badge, which read that she was a student from Eagle Point Community College.

"Do you get paid for being here?"

She hesitated before answering. "No. It's just for the clinical hands-on part of my training."

"You had to be here at what time?"

"Four. I'm an EMT student."

"Right. I remember you mentioning that now." That explained her having medical knowledge when she'd kept him informed on his flight home from Afghanistan. He remembered that he'd intended to explain heart rhythm abnormalities to her.

Jack studied her tired eyes and drawn features. "What time do you have to work until?"

Her eyebrows furrowed. "Just until eight."

No wonder she was tired all the time. "How many days per week do you do this?"

She folded arms across her chest in what he'd come to know as her defensive maneuver. "Why are you interrogating me, Jack? I don't see how this is any of your business."

He'd been asking because he was concerned about her, and her health and well-being. But he didn't want her knowing that just yet, for some reason. Nor that he was capable of kindness, thoughtfulness and genuine care for the people around him.

No, he wasn't ready to show that side of himself to Olivia just yet.

"If it negatively impacts your work at the diner, it *is* my business."

Her countenance deflated and he wished he hadn't been so harsh.

"I try very hard not to let that happen," she said with the kind of edge that gave him the distinct impression she was on the verge of either tears or clobbering him. Maybe both.

Her eyes avoided him in favor of studying his dad. "So, he seems to be resting okay?"

"Yeah, now. He had a reaction to a medication. Amoxicillin."

Her jaw dropped. "What? How? They knew he was allergic to penicillin."

"I didn't." That Olivia knew dinged Jack's ego. "How did you know that?"

"He told me all of his medical history, in case of an emergency. I told the paramedics. They wrote it on the chart." She shook her head. "This should never have happened."

Jack motioned her to the hallway where he flagged down a nurse and inquired. She confirmed after comparing the input record to Sully's hospital chart. "Miss Abbott is correct. The allergy is listed here. It didn't get transcribed onto his hospital chart." The nurse looked distressed and highly disturbed about it, as did Olivia. Which meant someone was in trouble.

While Jack fought anger at the staff person responsible for the error, he also knew people weren't perfect and that he'd needed enough grace of his own, especially early in his military career.

Yet, those weren't the only thoughts occupying his mind.

Intruding somewhere in the middle of the medication muddle, a part of him was touched by the fact that Olivia had the presence of mind to tell the paramedics about the penicillin allergy.

Which could only mean that his father meant more to her than Jack had first realized.

Olivia had made enough mistakes of her own to know the important part was owning up. She felt bad for the person who'd made the error, yet concern for Sully outweighed it. A mistake like that could kill someone. Precisely the reason Olivia needed to be sure and study hard so she didn't make a similar mistake once on the job. She wanted to be a good EMT.

Jack, however, looked ready to take someone's head off.

"Thankfully it didn't affect Sully's airway," she said to tame Jack's temper. "Just hives." She knew because one of Sully's nurses had been kind enough to keep her updated from the report. She hadn't known that the offending drug was amoxicillin, though. Just that he'd reacted.

"But the next time could be life threatening," Jack said more to Olivia than the nurse.

"Can I see his chart?" Olivia asked the nurse, who looked at Jack. He narrowed his gaze at Olivia but nodded. Olivia read over Sully's allergies and her concern grew. Not one of Sully's many allergies had made the transfer from the ambulance chart to the medical record. Jack was absolutely going to freak…and for good reason.

Olivia kept her voice even as she handed the nurse back the chart and said, "The rest of his allergies aren't listed here. Please make sure his new family doctor and all future caregivers know Sully also has a severe allergy to shellfish."

"Which means he can't take sulfa drugs," the nurse said, scribbling notes down. Olivia avoided Jack's searing gaze. He had no reason to be angry with her. She hadn't created this problem. In fact, she was fixing it. He ought to be grateful. Instead, he looked grumpy. Maybe with himself?

"Anything else?" the nurse asked Olivia, turning her back slightly to Jack.

Olivia wished the nurse wouldn't face away from Jack. That wouldn't go over well.

"Yes," Olivia said, trying to position herself to bring Jack back into the circle of conversation. "He also reacts to pecans and bananas. His skin breaks out with certain Band-Aids and blisters if he touches rubber bands. So I suspect he has a contact latex allergy as well, though Sully denies it."

A doctor Olivia had never seen before approached and joined the conversation as the nurse compared the records.

"To be on the safe side, we probably need to list latex as an allergy," the doctor said.

The nurse added, "We're latex-free here at this facility, so he should be fine. But some smaller facilities still use latex in some supplies."

That the doctor and nurse were telling Olivia all of this and not Jack appeared to be frustrating him beyond belief. His eyebrows were scrunched together and he had that telltale set to his jaw. The doctor extended the clipboard toward Olivia. "Can you sign this form?"

"Excuse me, I'm Sully's medical power of attorney," Jack said firmly, eyeing the doctor.

"Oh, my mistake. Miss Abbott just seemed to know more. You are…?"

"His son."

The doctor gestured between Olivia and Jack. "Are you two related, then? Married?"

Jack and Olivia shot several steps away from each other.

"No!"

Absolutely not!"

The doctor's eyebrows rose. "Well, all righty then. Divorced?"

Jack scowled.

Olivia glared at both of them. Then, feeling a blush creep up her neck and into her face at the thought of being married to Jack, she turned to go start her shift.

"Not funny, Edna," Olivia said to the medical records clerk as she snickered and snorted in the corner. Edna had evidently heard the hallway exchange and found it humorous.

"You should've seen Jack's face. He looked about to blow a gasket."

"Don't tick him off. I have to work with him at the diner."

"Right. Lucky you."

"You're funny."

"No, I mean it. He's a cutie. I'd put up with his rigid, rule-following, no-compromise, no-nonsense, military personality just to be able to stare at him for a few hours. Guy's gorgeous and built like a tank."

Olivia rolled her eyes. "He's young enough to be your grandson."

"He's not too old for *you*, though." Edna winked dramatically.

"That's so ridiculous it's obscene." The notion that she'd *ever* be remotely interested romantically in Jack or he in her? Nonsense.

That she'd blushed around him all day during that last shift at work just had to do with the heat being on full blast in the diner because of the customers being cold and nothing more.

By the time her shift ended a few hours later, Olivia was ready to drop. Her feet felt as if they had blisters on the bottoms of them. She groaned and stretched her achy back.

"A bunch of us are heading out to catch a flick at the dollar show. You coming?" Edna asked.

"Thanks, but I have to skip it. I still have to pick up some supplies before the next storm hits."

"All right then. Catch you later."

Olivia waved to her nutty but adorable elder friend and then said goodbye to nurses Kate, Lauren and Caleb and doctors Mitch, Ian, Cade and the rest of the trauma crew that had graciously taught her so much on incoming trauma cases tonight. She needed to get some ride-along hours with the ambulance service next semester. She really looked forward to that.

She pushed open the EPTC door to frigid wind. She pulled her coat tighter and braved the snowy parking lot. Midway, she spotted Jack's Ford. An idea formed.

Unable to resist jabbing him and continuing the good-natured ribbing over liking opposing car makes, she pulled out her notebook and a roll of bandage tape from her medical bag. She wrote FORD=Found On Road Dead next to the Ford emblem on the truck where he'd see it. "And we score one point, Sully," she whispered toward his hospital room window. Then, snickering to herself, she hurried to her car, looking forward to the warmth of the heater. She turned the ignition over.

Nothing.

Whaaaat?

She pulled the key out and tried again. Nothing. No sound whatsoever. Just a dead click.

"You have got to be kidding me." She tried again. Still nothing.

"Come on, you silly car." Olivia tried unsuccessfully for several more moments before going out and opening her hood. She knew quite a bit about the engine and fiddled around with it but couldn't find the issue. Everyone from her EMT class had left, so she couldn't bum a ride. She peered over at the trauma center as two ambulances pulled in, shooting down her idea to go inside and ask for a hand with her car.

She could go in and offer to stay but she was too new to actually be of help and would only be in the way.

Eagle Point didn't currently have a cab service or she'd call one. So she called a wrecker instead.

With a groan of dread, she slammed her hood, grabbed her purse, bundled up as best she could and started walking.

It wasn't cold enough yet that she'd freeze to death or get frostbite.

She'd just be uncomfortable…and extremely tired. It was only about a four-mile walk from the trauma center to the diner. The walk wouldn't be pleasant, but it wouldn't kill her, either.

She really needed things from the store before the big ice storm hit tomorrow, the main item being her emergency asthma inhaler from the store's pharmacy. The store was closer to ten miles away though. She shouldn't risk it.

She studied her inhaler. Still a few puffs left. That would get her through for now.

Once home, she'd just have to call a friend or neighbor to get her inhaler for her or to give her a ride. Because Olivia grew up in poverty, she hated asking for handouts, even rides.

She'd much prefer to be the one helping than the one needing help.

Lord, I'm trying not to feel sorry for myself here.

She pulled out her phone and left a message for Patrice, to see if she could get a ride. Darin had an old DUI and couldn't drive. And Naem was probably babysitting his sister's babies tonight, as usual. She'd call if she got too cold.

A long miserable mile down the road her teeth were chattering, darkness was closing in and her legs were stiff and sore. Hopefully Patrice would call back soon. Her muscles quivered from the cold and trying to keep her small frame warm.

And she couldn't stop coughing and feeling bronchospasms. She'd used her inhaler but on the second pump, unfortunately, found it empty. The gauge must have been off.

The sound of a vehicle approaching echoed in the road behind her. Not comfortable riding with strangers, and embarrassed at her predicament, she tried to wave it on but the person seemed to be slowing down, probably intending to stop. She pulled her scarf away from her cheek so she could see who was pulling up beside her. She prayed it was someone she knew. She peeked.

Definitely someone she knew.

In fact, it was the last person she'd want finding her like this.

Jack Sullenberger pulled over right ahead of her...in the Ford she'd just made fun of.

Why was that woman walking at dusk in weather like this? Jack wondered. Something about her and the way she moved seemed very familiar.

Spiky tresses were tucked into a bright red beanie, stark against her black hair, and she wore matching red lipstick. Walking rapidly, she hunched her shoulders against the falling snow and dipped her head, probably to shield it from the wind.

Jack backed up so she wouldn't have to walk so far to get to his truck. He stepped out and realized why she seemed familiar.

"Olivia," he said, shocked. Her face was pale, her cheeks were red and her respirations were puffing out too rapidly for his liking. "What's going on?"

"Just on my way home," she said, voice strained...

"I see that. Why are you walking?"

She paused in front of him and pursed her lips.

Why wouldn't she tell him? Then it dawned on him. Her car had evidently broken down. "Need a lift?" he asked as nonchalantly as possible since she seemed embarrassed.

She waved—more like waved him off, shoulders scrunched. Her breath wheezed out in white, wispy mists in front of her. "I'm fine."

"Look, I'm going that way anyway." A lie, but so be it.

"I'd p-prefer to walk." She shivered and the words warbled out. She started to walk around him.

Concern caused him to step in front of her. He leaned in. Did the skin around her lips and eyes look blue? Or was that the lighting? No, her skin was pale and slightly dusky. Her breaths were coming faster and seemed shallow compared to a moment ago.

"Get in the truck, Olivia." He really hoped she wouldn't make him pick her up and put her in there against her will. He was half tempted to take her back to the trauma center.

She stopped and stared at him, apparently not liking being told what to do.

"Don't test me," he said with a heavy warning in his tone as he opened the door wider.

"Fine." With a grunt, she let him help her in. He went to the driver's side and got in.

After buckling up, she folded her hands stiffly in her lap and stared straight ahead.

"Thank you," she said in a resigned voice a few moments later. Her teeth chattered and she still trembled from the cold. Or maybe from having to take a ride from him.

This would be funny if Jack weren't so concerned about her safety out in this weather alone. He had a lecture on the tip of his tongue, but she didn't look ready to hear it.

"Do we need to call a wrecker for your Chevy?" Jack tried not to smirk. He really did.

Because he was paying attention to traffic, he didn't see her glare, but boy he could feel it as her head whipped around exorcist-style. "That's not funny. And I already called a tow truck. They didn't answer but I left a message."

Her color was a little better now that she was inside the warmth of his truck.

He turned the heater up high, noticing the scrap of paper he'd written Perry's number and home address on. He turned it over so she wouldn't see it. No one needed to know he'd reached out to Perry and was trying to help him straighten out his life.

Jack hated to see a young man destroy himself with bad choices. If he could stop it, he would. Until he returned overseas, he could try to be a positive influence on Perry, who enjoyed working out and watching ball games on television. Jack had taken him to a hockey game last weekend and they'd been working out together. Perry had seemed thankful.

Olivia coughed beside him, drawing Jack from his reverie.

"You're wheezing."

"Asthma. It's exercise-, cold- and stress-induced. Apparently snow-induced, as well."

"Do you have your inhaler with you?"

"I'm embarrassed to admit I let it run out. I'd have gone to pick up the prescription if my car hadn't broken down. I've been using my inhaler more than usual the past couple of months. This semester has been tough."

He nodded, knowing she didn't need to be scolded. "Which pharmacy?"

She faced him now, looking as though she was about to protest, but her breathing really was labored. Her shoulders relaxed in resignation. "The one in Eagle Point Grocery Mart."

He was glad she was drifting back to the side of sense. "Since we're closer now to that than the trauma center, we'll go on ahead." Otherwise, he'd have taken her to the trauma center for an asthma treatment. At this point, it would be faster to get her inhaler from the pharmacy. If she showed any sign of worsening, he'd pull over and call an ambulance. Driving someone to the hospital in a true emergency was not wise. Her color was okay. Not ideal, but not life threatening, either. The cold must've given her skin that blue hue.

She shifted uncomfortably. "I didn't realize my inhaler was so low, or I'd have asked one of the doctors to give me an emergency inhaler from the EPTC pharmacy. Besides, the attack didn't happen until about a mile down the road. Right before you came along, actually."

He nodded, not wanting to add to her stress or increase her body's need for oxygen.

"I understand," he said, sensing how embarrassed she was about her unintended lapse. "Believe it or not, I'm glad to help."

He couldn't believe he just admitted that, but he didn't want her out walking in the cold. In fact, it bothered him more than he cared to admit that she hadn't felt she could call him for help. "Olivia, you have my cell number if you ever need help or anything. Feel free, okay?"

She grew very quiet, then shot him a quick side glance before saying softly, "Okay."

He hoped she would. "The ice storm is going to be bad. What else do you need while we're out? Makes sense to pick stuff up while we're here. Anything you'd need for a week."

"I need to pick up a few grocery-type things, if you don't mind, before you take me home. If it's not an inconvenience."

"Not at all. When do you have clinical again?"

"Every other day, on weekdays. Monday, Wednesday and Friday of one week, then Tuesday and Thursday of the next week. Then class every day I don't have clinical, except Sunday. Unless they cancel it due to inclement weather."

"I can give you rides until you get your car fixed. I go to the trauma center to see Dad every day, anyway.

It makes sense for you to simply ride with me. I usually stay a few hours in the evening, visiting with him. So I'll just leave when your shift ends."

There was a moment of silence and then, "Thank you."

"I can give you rides to class, too, if you need it."

She shook her head. "I usually do it from the computer at home. Occasionally we have to go to the college for things, but my car should be fixed by then. Speaking of that, I need the number for another tow truck. The first one didn't call me back."

"Call Eagle Point Wrecker Service. An old high school buddy owns it as well as a mechanic service. He'll cut you a break on both. Tell him I told you to call him."

"Okay. I appreciate it." She seemed embarrassed to need help. He felt badly for her. Yet he wasn't really keen on the idea of anyone knowing how much he really cared about people. It made him feel not in control and vulnerable.

As they drove, Olivia received a call from the pharmacy that her prescription was ready for pickup, so Jack figured she must have called it in while she was walking. Good. That would save time.

"What made you decide to be an EMT?" Jack asked, unsure whether he truly wanted to know or whether he was just trying to make conversation to help her be less on edge around him. Not to mention calming her down until she could take another dose of her asthma medication.

She explained the dream of working in trauma care that she'd had since childhood. She shared so freely that Jack used it as an in for the next thing he wanted to talk about, something he'd been wondering about for a while now. "You were going to talk to me about something personal back at the diner, one of the last times we were in the office."

She grew quiet—he could swear he heard her walls go up. "It's nothing, really. So, what about you? When did you know you wanted to be in the military?"

Her maneuver of changing the subject told him she no longer felt comfortable with whatever personal revelation she'd planned to tell him at the diner. He hoped she'd come around eventually, because he could tell it was really weighing on her.

He shared the how, why, where and when of his enlistment, and segued into his knowledge of trauma care. He talked about Sully and explained the different heart rhythm abnormalities. The change in her body language astonished him. She sat straighter, eagerly listening as all guardedness vanished. He realized what a great listener she was and how much of a delight she was to talk to. Moreover, he realized just how much he'd craved and missed this type of feminine companionship.

Best to change the subject and get things back on an impersonal track.

Somewhere in the mix of warm, lively conversation, he'd forgotten he was only asking to make conversation and distract her from her breathing. He couldn't even pinpoint when he'd become genuinely interested in hearing what she had to say. It troubled him a little that it had happened so naturally and so fully. Troubled him even more that he hadn't felt himself cross that self-drawn line until it was too late.

In the grocery store parking lot, snow crunched beneath Jack's boots as he went around to help her out. But by the time he reached her side of the truck, she'd stepped out of it. He held her elbow to steady her on the slick surface nonetheless. She stiffened at his touch but he didn't want her to fall.

He wished she didn't feel she had to present such a tough image around him, but the truth was she *was* tough. He didn't know many who'd work as hard as she did for an education and for a job. To the point of walking miles in the bitter cold and snow. He admired her.

Right now that was all he was willing to admit.

Jack shut the door and tightened his hold on Olivia. The wind picked up, swirling flakes in their midst. Though cold, the landscape was nicely dusted in snow. Passing the truck to grab two carts so workers would have fewer to collect, he noticed something fluttering on the front of his truck. He bent to read it, which was when Olivia turned from watching the snowfall to notice him.

"It stuck!" Olivia gasped. Then she giggled. He looked at her, too thrilled for words at the sweet and unexpected sound. He picked up the note, read FORD=Found On Road Dead and burst out laughing. Carts carving side-by-side paths in the inch of white powder, they took turns chuckling all the way to the doors. A strange sense of camaraderie connected them in the humor.

"I can't believe that note stayed on there," she said. "Good old bandage tape."

"I bet you just hate this, the fact that you had to ride in the dreaded Ford."

"I bet you just love this." She mimicked him, with a half smile, half smirk.

His hearty chuckle became the answer, and when Olivia's laughter joined his, a part of him realized that he'd do almost anything to hear it again.

Trouble.

That's what she was. Trouble. A distraction from his concentration and his regimented existence and rigid plans, plans that could not be broken, not even to enjoy a lady's company. He glanced her way and got caught up in the twinkle of dark, alluring eyes.

He swallowed and jerked his gaze away.

She grew quiet beside him and he knew she'd picked up on his backtracking.

Heading straight to the pharmacy, Olivia picked up her prescription and took a puff from her inhaler. Then they quickly gathered their groceries and the things Jack needed for the diner. He paid for it himself, to try and help get Dad caught up. Jack also put nonperishable food items in for Darin, since he'd caught glimpses of bare cabinets and an empty fridge after he'd given Darin a ride home yesterday when Naem couldn't. Darin had apologized profusely and been embarrassed for not having any refreshments to offer Jack, even though Jack hadn't minded. He felt badly for the guy, trying so hard for a better life.

Jack could only hope Perry would eventually do the same.

Jack and Olivia checked out and maneuvered their fully loaded carts toward Jack's truck. The snow fell in sheets now. "Go ahead and get in," Jack told her once they were back at his truck after starting the ignition so she'd be warm. "I'll load the groceries."

Surprisingly, she complied. The temperature had dropped so severely, he couldn't be more grateful that he'd seen her along that road or she'd still likely be walking. As Jack loaded the bags, he tried not to think about what would have happened if he hadn't come along when he did.

It was very telling of her interests and eating habits, seeing the sorts of things she bought. Mostly vegetables, then fruit, tons of cereal and butter pecan ice cream, his favorite kind. Until now, he had never met another person who ate it, especially in wintertime. The odd little commodity commonality made him feel a bit strange in terms of uniquely and unexpectedly bonding over something as silly as ice cream. He had some in his cart, too, and he'd doubted she noticed at the time. But at the truck, she'd seen it in his bag and grinned while eyeing him with a peculiar sort of winsome interest.

He'd be better off not thinking about it, or about how pretty her dark eyes and deep dimples were when she smiled like that. Nor how his heart rate kicked up upon seeing it.

Once in the truck and back on the road to the diner, Jack thought of the little message she'd written and then the fact that her car, rather than his, had broken down. He chuckled again when she made a mock-sour face and stuck her tongue out at him.

"How are you enjoying riding in a Ford while your Chevy is dead on the side of the road?"

He stopped at a red light, and Olivia aimed a finger at him. "Jack Sullenberger, you tell anyone, and I mean *anyone*, that I rode in a Ford and I'll deny it to my death." She was laughing by the end of the sentence and the sound of it sent another pleasant thrill through him. He'd like to hear her laugh more. That could lead to problems.

Jack realized something else that was concerning. The longer he was around her in a nonwork setting, the less they squabbled and the more she appealed to him.

He needed to focus on keeping his guard up.

He'd made it this far unaffected by her and he wanted to keep it that way. Otherwise there was no telling what might happen.

Chapter Six

"So, what's up with Jack bringing you home last night?"

Olivia cringed at Patrice's question, coming from behind her in their apartment kitchen. She couldn't explain what happened last night with Jack to herself, never mind to anyone else. Not that anything had really *happened*.

"My car broke down and he gave me a ride is all." She slowly turned in her chair. When she saw the bruise on Patrice's cheek she forgot all about the question and gasped. "What happened to you?"

Patrice cuddled her coffee cup tighter and turned away from Olivia. "Nothing."

Olivia shot out of her chair, rushed across the linoleum floor and turned Patrice around as gently as she could. "Did he hit you?" Olivia had always suspected Patrice's boyfriend of being abusive.

Now she knew.

Patrice set her coffee mug down. Her hands were shaking.

"You need to get away from him."

Patrice shrugged and turned away. "I started the argument."

"That doesn't give him the right to harm you."

Patrice whirled around. "I never said he harmed me. Don't go spreading that around. I mean it."

"You told me he shook you and made you bite your tongue. That constitutes harm."

"Leave it be, Olivia."

"No. You look me in the eye and tell me he didn't hit you in the face."

Patrice's shoulders sank. She stayed silent and shook her head as a tear trickled down her cheek. Olivia gave her a hug, which is when she noticed new bruises on Patrice's arms, too. "What happened here?" she whispered. "Please tell me."

"He grabbed me by the arms and shook me again," Patrice whispered back.

Olivia sighed, knowing it was very difficult for most women to leave their abusers. "We need to get you away from him."

Patrice licked her lips. "I can't. He's an attorney. He says he'll destroy me, my future."

Olivia clenched her jaw. "Come to church with me, Patrice. We have counselors there. You need to know there is a life beyond this abuse, and that you can do better than this creep. Jesus will never hurt you," Olivia whispered, her tears mirroring Patrice's.

"I don't know if I can. I've done so much. You don't even know."

"Never too much to be forgiven."

"I'm a mess, Olivia. I'm not like you."

"You don't have to get cleaned up before you come to God. Come as you are and He will help you work on the things He wants changed. I suspect that, rather than tell you everything you're doing wrong, God will make sure you see everything right about you. And that you know His mercy above knowing your mistakes. You can trust Him."

Patrice peered into Olivia's eyes. "I sure hope you're right. Because I'm pretty sure you'd hate me if you knew some of the mistakes I've made."

"I'd never hate you." Although stark concern ran through Olivia. What had Patrice's boyfriend gotten her into? "But you need to tell someone, Patrice. Someone in authority."

Patrice sniffled and drew a deep breath. "I'll look up numbers for counselors or something. For now, let's get my mind off this stuff, okay? It's depressing and dismal. How about we work on the mitten project?"

Olivia gave her one more hug and smiled, even though her smile felt thin. She felt as if Patrice was just saying that about the counseling to appease Olivia. But, perhaps if she let Patrice calm down, she could get through to her at a later time.

"Making mittens sounds good, I guess."

Patrice pulled the box of winter sweaters down and they picked a couple out in order to make several sets of mittens out of the old sweaters, a project they'd thought of to help the diner.

A knock sounded at the door several minutes later.

"If that's Darin and Naem, they're an hour early," Patrice said, looking at the clock.

They'd all planned to go sledding today, since the diner and most all of the businesses in town were closed due to the ice storm knocking out electricity in various places all over Eagle Point.

Olivia reached the door and opened it. Jack stood on the other side with a box.

"Hey. The delivery truck left this on my stoop yesterday, but it's yours. I didn't notice the name before or I'd have brought it sooner."

"Thank you," Olivia said, and stepped aside in case he wanted to enter.

He didn't make a move to. He nodded a greeting at Patrice as she passed by on the way to the kitchen.

She waved and quickly turned, probably to hide her bruise. At the angle in which she'd been standing, Jack probably hadn't seen the bruise or he'd have certainly said something. Olivia knew that for sure.

Maybe Jack needed to know about it. In fact…

"Jack, would you like to come in for hot cocoa?" She didn't want to betray Patrice's trust, but neither did she want her to be hurt worse. She also didn't want to be rude to Jack or make him feel left out. Plus, if Jack saw the bruise, perhaps he'd talk sense into Patrice.

He peered at the burgundy sweater and the baby blue mittens in Olivia's hands so she said, "We're making these mittens out of old sweaters people were going to throw away." She showed him a finished set of sweater-made mittens and then a set in progress.

"Nice salvage," Jack said. He sent a questioning look to Olivia when Patrice scurried to her room. Should Olivia tell Jack about the assault? Why hadn't Patrice called police?

"Everything okay?" Jack asked, and nodded toward Patrice's closed door.

Olivia shook her head. "Not really," she whispered.

Jack shifted from one foot to the other. "Anything I can do?"

"I'm not sure yet." Olivia peered back at Patrice's door. "I'll let you know."

He nodded.

That he just stood there awkwardly caused Olivia's

compassion to bubble. He spent so much time by himself. She suddenly felt compelled to include him in their diner crew outing. "We're all going sledding later. Naem was going to ask you to join us."

"He did. I appreciate the invitation, but I can't."

"Oh? Do you have something that needs to be done at the diner today? If so, we can help instead of go sled—"

"No. I don't need help with anything today. Enjoy your rare day off."

So, why didn't he want to go with them, then?

Olivia tried to shove away the feeling of being slighted or snubbed.

But Jack wasn't a snob, so this was something else. What?

As she studied him more thoroughly, he shifted, then glanced back toward Patrice's bedroom door. "So, you'll let me know if you guys need me?"

Olivia nodded, but felt weird about it now, as opposed to a moment ago. Clearly, Jack didn't want to hang out with them on a friendship basis. Yet he was concerned about Patrice.

Weird. Did he carry some kind of torch for her?

According to Patrice, he never had. Nor had she for him.

Maybe Jack carried that kind of concern for everyone. If so, she didn't know him at all.

Olivia's cell phone rang as Jack set the box inside her door and turned to go. She picked up the box feeling aggravated and confused. Jack Sullenberger did that to her.

"Hello?" Olivia shut her door while answering the call from her EMT instructor. Two minutes into the conversation, her heart sank and her knees grew weak. "What do you mean I failed both tests?"

Nausea accosted her and with it a sinking sensation

that her best would never be good enough. She'd grown up feeling that way and couldn't shake it now, the heaviness of insurmountable odds and old ineptitudes she felt incapable of overcoming.

She'd studied so hard and so long! Determination took hold of Olivia. Failure was not an option. She needed to study harder. Period.

And, somehow, get more rest. But that seemed like an unattainable dream at this point. Especially with Jack's new mandatory hours and meetings.

She had to tell Jack.

"Thank you for the grace in letting me retest," Olivia said to her instructor. "I appreciate it. I'll try not to let you down this time." She hung up feeling thankful her instructor believed in her enough to let her take the tests again. Now she just had to figure out where she'd gone wrong.

Hearing Patrice arguing on the phone, probably with Frankie, and knowing Darin and Naem were coming over soon, Olivia gathered her books and prepared to go study at her favorite corner booth in the diner. Being there reminded her of Sully. She missed him badly. He'd have the words of advice and encouragement she'd need to keep going.

Right now, she felt as if passing EMT school was going to be utterly impossible.

All things are possible with You, Lord. But maybe this was my dream and not Yours. Nevertheless, if it's Your will for me to help people, please help me pass these tests. I don't want my instructor to be disappointed in me after she's given me grace.

Olivia wrote a note for her friends saying that she wouldn't be able to go sledding, after all.

She knew they planned, after sledding, to stop by the cabins next to the trauma center to work on the one its owner was donating to EPTC. It would be used by families of trauma victims who needed a place to stay overnight or for several nights. She wrote that she'd try to stop by the cabin and help if she could. It was a good cause. Something the community desperately needed. Especially people from out of town, since Eagle Point really didn't have a hotel or short-term housing options. She'd heard someone was planning on building a small housing community and some apartment complexes soon. Though that may have just been unfounded rumor, she hoped it would happen.

She gathered her schoolbooks and headed down to the darkened diner with a battery-operated lamp, fully intent on spending the rest of the day and evening studying her guts out.

The third time Jack heard the clattering before dawn the next morning he knew he wasn't imagining it.

Someone was downstairs rummaging around the diner.

He took the safety off his firearm and tiptoed down the stairs. When he saw Olivia halfway in the cabinet under the sink, he put the safety back on and slid the pistol into its hip holster. "Olivia," he said.

She jerked upright, hitting her head on the frame of the sink cabinet opening. "Ow. Yes?"

He raised his brows. "How did you get in here, and what are you doing?"

"Taking a break from studying to fix the sink."

He stepped closer. Sure enough, she'd repaired the drain. Quite nicely, in fact.

He'd seen the drain supplies in her grocery cart yesterday but had no idea she'd bought it for the diner. "I can reimburse you for that stuff…as well as the time you spent working on this."

"Not necessary," she said standing. "It didn't cost much or take long."

"Olivia—"

"Sully's worth it, Jack. The diner means a lot to me, as does your dad. I don't want or need to be reimbursed. I'm perfectly capable of making my own way."

The stubborn set to her jaw and the warning flash in her eyes told him it was no use arguing with her. She wasn't going to budge on this one. He shook his head.

Then he recalled the other thing she said. "You're studying…down here?"

She gestured toward the booth in the corner. "I always do. Patrice likes to have loud, obnoxious people over and I really don't like her boyfriend and his friends." She bit her cheek, as though she'd said too much. And yet, not nearly enough.

He noted the two plates and cups stacked in the sink. "How long have you been down here?"

"All night. I paid for the meals I heated up." Her eyes scanned the toaster oven.

He glanced around, not sure how he felt about Olivia being here when he wasn't.

The vulnerable look in her eyes made him want to be civil.

"Did you guys have fun sledding yesterday?"

"They said they did. I didn't end up going, so Patrice texted me about how it went. You should have gone. The fun would do you good."

He studied her, wondering if she was implying he needed to lighten up.

He didn't agree. In order to maintain their respect in his authority, he felt he must draw lines between himself and them. To join in the fun would erase that line and Jack couldn't let that happen.

Plus, for his own reasons, he needed to have less fun with Olivia.

He swept his gaze around one more time, prioritizing in his mind which repair jobs needed to take precedence over others. Dad had really started to let the place go. Very unlike him. Again, guilt accosted Jack for not noticing his dad had been unwell. Scanning his eyes back across the diner, he noticed something else. The cash register drawer was ajar. He walked over, looked at it then turned to Olivia. "Was this open when you got here?"

Her eyes went to the register and widened. "No."

"Did you go in there?"

"Yes," she said. Then she went over and shoved it closed. He stepped in her path as she tried to walk away. "Why?"

"I'd forgotten to put something in," she said, nibbling her lip and avoiding eye contact.

"For the meals you ate here?"

"Yes, partly."

"Then why else were you in the register?"

"A good reason. Personal." She was beginning to perspire.

"Too vague." His temper was getting the best of him. First, she got into the register. Next, she thought she could justify not telling him why? No. Not happening. "Either tell me, or you are out of here. And I mean for good." His jaw was clenched as he seethed.

She met his gaze eye to eye now. "Jack, I didn't take anything out. You need to trust me." While her voice shook, she raised her chin, boldly holding his gaze. "Please."

He shook his head, not liking this at all. But to fire her now would probably upset his dad and hinder his recovery. Or worse, cause another stroke. "How did you get into the diner?"

"Your dad gave me the extra set of keys."

"The only extra set?"

"Yes." She tried to skirt around him but Jack held firm ground. If he stepped aside, she'd flee.

That his dad had given her the keys and no one else was more proof Sully trusted Olivia more than the others. Only now, with the register debacle, Jack wasn't sure his dad's judgment was sound after all.

Jack held out his hand. "Diner keys. I want them back. Now."

Her eyes flashed fury. She yanked the keys out of her jeans pocket and slapped them into his outstretched hand. Then she swerved from his presence, grabbed all of her books in one fell swoop and stormed past him, not bothering to make eye contact.

Maybe he should let her explain. But instead, he mentally berated himself for not counting the register before leaving the last time he was here. That was about to change.

"Olivia," he called up the stairs. She kept going.

"I want the keys to the register, too."

She stopped stiffly, then slowly turned. The look of bewilderment on her face gave him pause.

Without a word, she unhooked the tiny key from a wristlet key ring and flung it down to him before turning and shutting her door. That she did so calmly told him she was angrier than if she'd slammed it. He hadn't missed the confusion in her dark eyes.

For a moment, he considered asking for an explanation, but in his experience, people lied in these kinds of situations.

He went back to the diner to lock up and realized she'd

left her lamp there, shining brightly in the corner. He went to pick it up when he noticed a pamphlet she'd dropped.

He picked it up, not intending to read its contents, but National Dyslexia Foundation jumped out at him as though someone intended Jack to see it.

He turned the pamphlet over and read the first few lines, realizing it was reading tips and techniques to assist with comprehension and recall of material.

For those with dyslexia.

Was this something she was studying for school?

Or for herself, because she had the disorder?

He sighed, and felt like the world's biggest jerk. Then felt like the world's second biggest jerk when he saw Olivia's tip container empty. Why had she brought it in here?

He went to the register and counted out bills.

Was Olivia taking money out?

Or putting money in?

Moreover, why had he automatically thought the worst of her?

Jack shook his head, disgusted with himself and his mistrust of people.

But there was more at stake, more to lose if he trusted her and she wasn't worthy of it, than if he didn't trust her and she did deserve it. Right?

His main goal, first and foremost, was to get the diner out of the red.

He couldn't do that until he made sure no one was stealing money. So, for that reason, he'd err on the side of not trusting anyone completely.

And that included Olivia.

Chapter Seven

"**J**ack really blessed me, man," Darin said to Naem while he turned on the new grill a few days after the ice storm cleared. "Surprised me, too, that he brought all those groceries by. He's so hard-core here, I didn't know the dude had it in him to be nice off the job."

Olivia gritted her teeth at the chatter regarding Jack. Naem and Darin had been going on and on about Jack ever since getting here this morning. That they'd all come to work to the sight of new grills and coffeemakers had set a jovial mood among the crew. She had a feeling Jack paid for those items out of his own pocket. But why did he feel the need to do nice things at a distance?

She was glad for Darin, glad that he had a stocked pantry and fridge. But her feelings were still hurt over Jack's blatant mistrust.

He'd probably never believe she was putting her tips into the register, rather than taking money out of it. Now, without the keys, she couldn't put money in. Unless...

She sidled up next to Patrice. "I need a favor."

"What, sugar?" Patrice glanced sideways while tying her order pad apron on. This close, Olivia could see the faded yellowish-brown bruise on her cheek despite the thick mask of concealer Patrice had tried to use. "I've been putting my tips into the register, but since Jack took my keys, I can't. So when you open it, I need you to put my tips in at the end of the day. I need you to promise me you won't tell Jack. Or Sully if you go see him."

Patrice sighed. "Okay, if you promise not to tell them what Frankie did to me."

Concern coursed through Olivia. "No. I can't and won't promise that. Please tell me you're not still with him."

Patrice sighed and grabbed a stack of menus to distribute to tables. "I don't have time for this."

Naem came over to grab his order pad. "Why the sour look?"

Olivia shook her head. "I'm worried about Patrice for one thing. For another, Jack doesn't trust me."

"What makes you say that?"

Olivia really didn't want to get into it. "I just know."

"Hey, I know the guy's been rough on us, but he's actually pretty decent. He filled my tank up with gas and also left a gas card filled with money. For running diner errands he said, but I only drove, like, two miles."

"Does he know that?"

"Yeah. When I asked him about it, he told me he heard I drive my sister to all her doctor appointments and take her kids to school events and to their games and stuff, since she can't drive after her surgery. He heard about her cancer and how I help watch the kids for her after her chemo treatments."

"He's probably just doing that so you won't miss work here. I can't imagine Jack Sullenberger doing anything unless it benefits him," Olivia said, then wished the words back when Naem's eyes widened. His gaze settled behind her, over her right shoulder.

Heat of a presence bored into Olivia's back.

The hair on Olivia's neck stood on end. She read the answer in Naem's eyes.

Jack was standing right behind her.

Well, she may have just gotten herself fired, after all.

Her hands shook as she tied her apron on and tucked her order pad and pen into the pocket. Not turning around, she slid on noodle legs past Naem and out of Jack's presence, but she could still feel the weight of his stare on her back. She didn't turn around because she was scared of what she'd see.

She really needed to watch what she said.

She went to the door to turn the Closed sign to Open. Before she could, a hand covered hers.

"Wait."

Jack.

Olivia could barely breathe. He didn't seem mad. Just—urgent.

She swallowed and looked up.

For a second, she saw a pained expression. Then it disappeared, replaced by a rigid, blank steely slate that she couldn't begin to read.

"I need to talk to you in my office," he said.

"We open in ten minutes," she said, averting her gaze and hoping to deter him from this dreaded confrontation. Why, oh why, had she stupidly said something so insensitive and rude?

Probably because her feelings were still hurt over him stripping her of the keys. Not to mention his trust.

How mad was he? How far would he go to make her pay for her actions? Just this week, Jack had axed two evening-shift employees. One for reasons unknown, and the other had walked out after a verbal exchange with Jack. Her heart began to pound at the thought of losing her job. She should have been more careful to guard her thoughts and to tame her tongue.

She glanced humbly up to meet his gaze, knowing full well she was visually pleading.

"This will only take a few minutes." Without waiting for her, he turned to head to his office. A few minutes—what? To fire her? That's what she was afraid of.

She shook her head at herself and nibbled her lip, fighting a fiery blush.

Patrice, Darin and Naem all watched her follow Jack, their compassionate expressions stating the obvious. They were all afraid she was about to get chopped.

The urge to beg for her job hit Olivia. But her pride wouldn't let the words come.

Maybe Jack was right. Maybe she was too stubborn for her own good.

"Sit down." He indicated a chair as they entered the office. "Please," he added, almost as an afterthought. The fact that he seemed to be trying to smooth the rough edges off his usually surly manner of speech gave her a little ray of hope that maybe he'd have mercy on her and let her keep her job.

She sat, folded her arms in her lap and stared at the floor.

"What's going on with Patrice?" he asked.

Olivia looked up, startled.

Had he not called her in here because she'd gossiped about him?

"What do you mean?"

"The bruise on her face. Where'd she get it?"

Olivia swallowed. "She doesn't want me to say."

"But you think you need to?"

She nodded, eyeing the door and hoping Patrice wasn't listening.

"So, let me ask you this. How much do you know about her boyfriend?"

Relief flooded in over Jack's wisdom in not having Olivia directly say it. "Enough to know I don't like him. I also know he doesn't like us."

"Us?"

"Me, Darin, Naem—Patrice's diner friends. Or, at least, he doesn't approve of us."

"Guy sounds like a jerk."

"He thinks we're beneath him." Olivia shrugged. "Maybe we are."

"The world only works that way because people buy into the lie that it does. No one is less valuable than another person."

Jack's words left Olivia speechless, because they gave her a glimpse of nobility and character she never would have guessed he had. This glimpse gave Olivia a sense of security and rightness with telling him her knowledge about Patrice. It was really none of her business why Jack was so concerned.

A terrifying thought hit her. She wasn't jealous, was she?

Olivia shook herself out of that silly, out-of-nowhere notion. They had a mutual concern for Patrice. Her safety took priority over Olivia's secret wishes or insecurities. "This isn't the first time he has physically abused her."

Jack raked a hand across his military-style buzz. "The guy sounds like a real winner."

Should she tell Jack about the other bruises? He and Patrice were longtime friends. But if Jack told Patrice, she may not open up to Olivia the next time it happened. And he could end up putting her in the hospital or worse.

I don't know what to do, Lord. I just know I can't ig-

nore it or look the other way. I have to intervene and help her if she won't help herself.

She knew from Sully that in addition to being a combat medic, Jack was a longtime commander in the Air Force Security Forces. That meant he protected people, right? Maybe he could protect Patrice. At the risk of harming her and Patrice's friendship, Olivia whispered, "She has other bruises. On her arms, from where he shook her. That's happened twice that I know of."

Jack's face hardened. He nodded.

"Please don't tell her I said anything." She darted glances to the door.

Jack met Olivia's gaze. "If she's not willing to get away from him, there's not much we can do. You need to keep trying to get through to her, to maybe see a professional who can teach her about abuse cycles. In the meantime, please keep me informed."

The depth of concern in his face gave Olivia the impression he had a personal stake in Patrice's safety somehow. "I will." She waited to see if he had anything else to say, maybe about her earlier indiscretion, but he was quiet. Finally she asked, "Are you angry with me?"

He didn't look up. Just kept scrawling something on paper. Notes on supplies needed for repairs, from the looks of it.

"I mean, you'd have a right to be angry."

"And you have a right to your opinion," he stated simply, still writing.

Should she apologize for being rude? Then again, he still didn't trust her. And, it's not like he'd apologized for his part. Maybe it was best to just change the subject. She faced the clock. Five or so minutes until it was time to open the diner.

"Can I ask you a question?"

He peered up. Scowled slightly. "Proceed."

"Why did you fill up Naem's tank?" She really, really needed and wanted to know.

His mouth thinned. His gaze lifted to hers and then grew cold and steely. Formidable. He leaned forward slowly. Her breath caught. She wished she hadn't asked.

"Because he brings Darin to work and I *selfishly* want to make sure they make it to work on time," he bit out. Then narrowed his gaze as he held hers, daring her to say more about it.

Her mouth opened slightly, then she shut it.

Had his feelings been hurt by what she'd said? That would really surprise her. Jack Sullenberger with feelings or a slightly tender place in his heart?

Highly unlikely.

And yet, riding beneath the furrow of his manly brows a hint of something she could only describe as an ache resided. He held it in the tense gnawing of his jaw, firm and hard like his resolve. It suddenly hit her that he had many hidden facets. Ones she wanted to know about, for reasons she could not begin to fathom.

Now she was thoroughly and utterly confused. And pierced to the quick of her heart.

She'd started this day harboring resentment in her heart for his mistrusting, misunderstanding and misjudging her.

Now that she'd had a taste of her own medicine, it didn't feel very good.

"I'm sorry," she blurted.

He didn't flinch, didn't budge. Then after a moment, he slowly stood, not giving her any indication as to whether he accepted her apology or not, or if it meant anything to him.

She inched toward the door, feeling completely awkward.

"Olivia," he said softly. "One more thing."

His voice had a strangely tender ring to it.

She turned. "Yes?"

He slid the lime-green lamp and her Dyslexia Foundation pamphlet across the desk, holding her gaze the entire time.

Gulp. Had he read the pamphlet? Put two and two together?

She lifted her gaze from the lamp and pamphlet to his eyes.

The knowing light there, and the depth of understanding she never imagined she'd see in his face, told her... yes. She swallowed. Felt like looking down or away, but drummed up the courage not to. "Thank you," she said honestly. "If it's okay, I'll pick it up at the end of my shift."

He studied her a moment, then said, "Had you told me, I would have helped you." His voice was soft, and more compassionate than she'd thought him capable of.

She dipped her head low. "I don't want special treatment."

He came around the desk and stood so close she could feel the heat from his skin as he raked a strand of hair from her eyes. She blinked, startled at the nearness and the tenderness. "Olivia, if it helps you to study in the diner, so be it." Her breath hitched as his gaze inched down her face and then away. A jingling sounded, then he slid the extra set of diner keys atop her pamphlet. The significant gesture touched her more than he could know.

"Thank you," she said, trying to be grateful for the diner keys even though he didn't reinstate her register privileges. She understood his need to be watchful and cautious.

"It's nearly time to open. Please cover the initial customers and tell Patrice I need to see her in my office."

She nodded and turned to exit, knowing he was going to ask Patrice about the bruises.

She would be angry and think Olivia gave details.

But perhaps Jack could talk sense into Patrice, since they'd been childhood buddies.

He leaned around her to hold the door for her. His masculine cologne accosted her and reminded her of his alpha appeal. "You did the right thing by telling me."

"I hope so." She slowly lifted her gaze, searching his face but not knowing why. Their eyes met and locked in a moment of unguarded exploration. A sense of sweet wonder filled the space. A flash of overwhelming attraction hit Olivia that she was fairly certain reflected back in his eyes. So strong it felt as if all the air was siphoned from the room. Jack looked as perplexed as Olivia felt as they studied each other's faces as though they'd never seen them before.

Jack was first to turn away.

His uncompromising determination to remain aloof slid back into place, making Olivia wonder if she'd daydreamed the emotional exchange.

Yet the mutual magnetic pull had seemed so real, so alive, so filled with potential to thrive if even one of them gave in to it. Maybe it just had to do with feeling a bond because of a mutual concern for Sully and now Patrice. That had to be it.

Either way, she'd be better off not to dwell on it.

Even if there was something there, nothing between them would be remotely possible, in light of his eventual return overseas and her packed work, school and study schedule. Besides, the messages he'd sent were unmistakable. He didn't appear to be open to even friendship.

With gratitude for his grace and that her job was intact, she exited his office and went to wash her hands before work. The classic morning diner scents and sounds of sausage patties grilling, thick bacon frying, cheesy grits simmering, pepper-and-onion hash browns baking, eggs scrambling, Danishes heating, butter biscuits baking, maple syrup oatmeal bubbling and blueberry pancakes frying had never smelled and sounded so good.

He hadn't fired her. *This* time.

The next time she was unable to keep her mouth shut, he might not show the same mercy.

God, please help me see Jack the way You do. Lend me Your heart toward him and help me treat him the way You would, Lord. Sorry I let my anger and my mouth get away from me.

The lack of sleep from studying wasn't helping. In fact, the long-term sleep deprivation was altering her personality, obliterating her patience, erasing her self-control and making her crabby about dumb things. Plus, the coffee she'd nearly overdosed on to stay awake to study was making her jittery, anxious and edgy beyond belief.

Being in Jack's formidable—dauntingly handsome—presence only added to that.

So she should be content to avoid him, the way he avoided her.

After an uncomfortable moment of telling Patrice that Jack wanted to see her in his office, Olivia went to open the front door, glad to see customers heading toward the diner. A lot of customers. More than any other morning. Gladness filled her. She loved people, after all.

More business meant more revenue. Plus, staying busy would help her forget how disastrously the morning started.

It would also hopefully help her forget the warm feeling of protection that had washed over her the moment Jack had set his hand atop hers earlier, on this very sign.

She turned it over now, also turning over a new leaf in her heart symbolically.

Something in the flash of hurt in Jack's face—the part he hadn't quite been able to cover—no longer let her believe he'd acted selfishly with Naem as she'd thoughtlessly accused him of.

Then, there was his kindness in the wake of that, re-instating her free rein to study in the diner.

What should she do with the wonder rising up in her over the revelation that she may not know the real Jack Sullenberger? Likewise, what should she do with the seed of desire sprouting up? To want to know the real Jack, and perhaps be friends? She couldn't deny the draw. He seemed so much larger than life; he had makings of a true storybook hero behind his facade.

She was starting to see glimpses of the son Sully had talked about so much and so often that Olivia had felt like she'd known him. So why was Jack putting up this impenetrable front?

Because he didn't know her as well as she knew him. And she sensed there was more to know even still. More strength and goodness inside of the man than maybe even he comprehended.

Should she bury the intrigue and forget about it?

Or explore it?

Fortunately, she didn't have time to ponder further because the sidewalk had filled up with more people who filed in when she unlocked the diner doors.

Jack had been right. People were grateful for the early breakfast hours and were showing up.

She felt bad now for allowing Sully to hinder that by helping her with her hours. She needed to sacrifice her own needs for the greater good, for the community and for the diner.

If she failed, so be it. Somewhere along the way, it had become more important to her to save Sully's Diner than to succeed with EMT school. She'd love both, of course.

But the way things were going, both may not be possible. She'd quit school before she'd let these beloved, iconic diner doors close for good. She could always return to school later.

Lord, I pray it doesn't boil down to that hard choice. Make a way for each, if You will.

"Good morning," she said to the customers with a genuine smile. "Welcome to Sully's."

"You wanted to see me?" Patrice leaned in the doorway of Jack's office.

He motioned to the chair across the desk from him. "Please come in and sit down."

Patrice nibbled her lip while she closed the door and lowered herself nervously to the edge of the chair. "What's going on, Jack?"

"We've been friends a long time, Patrice." His jaw clenched. "Some would even say we're family."

She dipped her head before slowly looking back up. "Olivia doesn't yet know the history there, Jack, between my dad and your mom and the whole torrid affair. Please tell me you didn't say something to her about the possibility of us being half siblings."

"No. But if she's the great friend you say she is, I suggest you mention it to her."

Why Jack wanted Olivia to know he wasn't interested in Patrice, he had no idea. He just felt strongly that she needed to know. Or, rather, it was important to him that Olivia know.

He didn't want to ponder why.

Besides, that wasn't on today's agenda. "Are you going

to tell me what happened that led to your bruises? And, yes, I saw them."

She didn't need to know that he could barely detect the ones beneath her sleeves. He wanted to honor Olivia's wish that he not reveal her as the whistle-blower, only because he agreed with her that Patrice may then have a falling out with Olivia, and would be less protected and more isolated…which was probably her boyfriend's goal anyway.

The strong likelihood that Jack and Patrice were half siblings fueled his intent to protect her, even at the risk of making her angry. "Patrice. You're smarter than this."

She just looked away.

Jack hated that she'd been physically harmed, hated even worse that she'd been hurt emotionally. There was no fight left in her. None. Her eyes looked dead all the way to her soul.

"What's he done to you, sis?"

Her head whipped up. "Don't call me that until I have a chance to tell the crew, Jack."

He and Patrice had suspected for years that there was a chance they were half siblings. But not until recently had Patrice's dad and Jack's mom admitted to the near certainty that Jack's mom had, while estranged from Sully and toddler Jack, birthed Patrice. The baby had then been adopted and raised by her birth father and, graciously, his wife—her stepmother.

Jack suspected Sully knew, too, which is why he was so determined to watch over Patrice and provide for her, even though she wasn't his biologically. He had a soft spot for her.

She fiddled with her order pad apron. "I need to get back to work."

"What's it going to take to open your eyes, Patrice? I'd really hate to have to come ID your body at the morgue."

She gasped. "Don't say that!"

He leaned in. "Educate yourself on abusers and abuse cycles. The sooner you get away, the better chance you have of surviving. As it stands now, you've already died inside in so many ways." He felt a knot in his throat. "It breaks my heart. I fear for you. Don't make me take things into my own hands."

"Don't do something stupid and end up in jail, Jack."

"Then get help. And get out of the relationship. You know I can protect you."

She scoffed. "How? You'll be on another continent as soon as Sully recovers."

For the first time it hit Jack that going back to the military may not be the best thing.

She was right. If he wasn't here, he couldn't protect her.

"If you press charges, the legal system will handle him."

"No. I don't have faith in the justice system. Not with the stories he's told me as a defense attorney of how often criminals and domestic violence offenders get away with what they do and who pays who off in the process." Her eyes watered and spilled over. "Jack, I'm scared. I want to leave him. I do. Believe me."

"Did he threaten you?"

She nodded.

"Patrice, if you promise to get out and not go back, I'll help you. Can you do that?"

Patrice brought her gaze back to Jack, then to the floor.

"I can't promise you that today. I'd try, but I'm not strong enough yet."

Jack had never felt so frustrated in his life.

"Why put it off today, when you don't know what's going to happen tomorrow?"

"Jack, I will. I just need a plan first. Okay?"

He studied her, not completely happy but glad nonetheless that she seemed serious about coming up with an escape plan.

Her face softened. "I listened to you, Jack. Now I need you to listen to me for a second. I think you're making a huge mistake in not trusting Olivia," Patrice said as she stood. "Please reconsider."

The abrupt change in subject threw Jack for a loop. He didn't get the idea Patrice was just deflecting or changing the subject to get him off her back about getting away from her abusive boyfriend. Her face told him she was serious. Olivia must have mentioned their run-in with the register and him taking her keys. However, he felt justified in doing so.

Or had, until seeing her today. Even after he'd let her know he'd seen the pamphlet and that he was going to let her study in the diner, after all.

That moment of connection between them when they'd stared those few awestruck seconds into each other's eyes…very unexpected and strange, indeed.

He knew exactly what to do with it though: nothing.

"We'll see," Jack said honestly. Something about the entire cash register exchange still bothered him. If Olivia couldn't tell him the whole truth as to why she was in it, he couldn't trust her.

Later that day, after the breakfast rush and before the lunch rush, when he wouldn't be at risk of being needed, Jack scrubbed frustrated fists in his eyes and went to shut the office door.

He had some very tough calls to make—figuratively and literally.

After narrowing down job applicants, talking options with the bank and going over Dad's personal finances, as well as the finances at the diner, he was mentally exhausted. Unless a miracle occurred, Jack couldn't see any way to prevent the foreclosure. He'd had to switch directions and talk with other restaurant owners in town whom he knew would keep his situation under wraps, and see if they'd be interested in buying the diner. That would be the only way to save it at this point. He hated to take that route or to admit defeat, but he had to look at other options.

Right before lunch, Jack called a few people who'd put in applications and performed phone interviews. Out of the five or so, two stood out and he asked them to come in for a second, face-to-face interview, so he could go over the rules with them and gauge their dependability level. He really couldn't afford to hire anyone right now, but the current crew was already stretched too thin and it wouldn't be fair to them not to hire someone.

He was also going to revamp the duties, so that the new dishwasher he hired also bussed tables, to free up Naem, Patrice and Olivia as well as the servers on evening crew. And he was going to hire an actual host or hostess, who'd also be a cashier, so the servers' loads would be lightened.

Just after the lunch rush, a knock sounded on Jack's office door. He was glad for the intrusion. The books were giving him a royal headache.

Jack went to open the door, which he rarely closed. But he didn't want the staff to get wind yet that, as a last resort cushion, he was talking to other business owners about purchasing Sully's. At least that would give it a chance to stay open for the community. Dad would be crushed. But at this point, Sully still wasn't out of the woods yet from his stroke, had not even fully regained consciousness. The doctors were keeping him medically sedated so the swelling in his brain would have a chance to come down to a safe level.

When he opened the door, Darin, Naem, Patrice and Olivia stepped in with papers in their hands. He didn't think they were all pulling a mass resignation, because they all had goofy grins on their faces. His headache eased at the look of childlike anticipation on their faces.

"What's up, guys?"

They walked over and each set the papers on Jack's desk. He opened one, read something about the current accumulated vacation pay being forfeited to the diner. Confusion accosted him.

He looked up. "What's this? I don't understand."

The crew eyed one another, then Jack. "These are legal, notarized forms that we're forfeiting our vacation pay to help with the diner debt."

Jack stood. "What? You can't be serious." This was a bombshell, to say the least. While the gesture was amazing, Jack couldn't take their vacation time. "Sorry guys. I can't let you do this."

Olivia was first to stare Jack down. "We insist."

"We want to make this donation, Jack," Darin stepped forward. "It's no use arguing."

Jack studied their faces. "You're serious."

"Dead," Naem said. Then grinned. "Come on, man, take a breath."

Jack did take a breath, then studied the papers and the sacrificial givers in front of him. "I don't know what to say."

"Say you'll accept it, or it'll hurt our feelings," Patrice said. Then she elbowed Olivia. "It was Olivia's idea, by the way, but we all jumped at the chance. Your dad has done a ton for us."

"As have you," Darin reminded him. "So just say thanks and get our boots back to work."

Jack laughed at that. *Get your boots back to work* was a phrase he used often. They were beginning to know him so well. He actually had to swallow past a pretty significant lump in his throat as he met each worker's gaze. "Thanks, sincerely. This means a lot." It would mean the world to Sully. Jack's heart broke that their sacrifice may not be enough.

That they were so willing to give made Jack want to pray that God would make a way for their sacrifice to be enough, somehow.

But he had trouble praying and believing in God's goodness after all he'd seen overseas.

"This means more than you'll ever know," Jack said. And he determined all the more to do whatever it took to save the diner, and to at least keep their jobs intact if the diner had to change owners in order to survive the debt eating it alive and causing the bank to threaten foreclosure.

"Thanks for accepting the gifts," Olivia said and motioned the crew back to work.

Jack sat stone still for the next several moments, as the weight of their kindness set in

I know I haven't talked to You regularly in a real long time, Lord. But, I know You see what they've done and I know You know what a true sacrifice that forfeiting these hours and this pay is. Bless them.

It almost made Jack want to go to church again. Almost.

Images of a different church, smoldering after a blast, hit Jack. The sounds rumbled through his bones. The screech of a missile that reached the walls before his warning. The impact. Being knocked to the ground only to look up and see the building obliterated. Shoes of the devout shredded from impact, scattered around him. No survivors. The parishioners who'd once protected his unit during ambush—gone.

"Jack? Everything all right, buddy?"

Jack jerked at the sound of Darin's voice. He swabbed sweat off his brow. "Yeah."

"Flashback?"

"Think so."

"Take a second." Darin nodded to the back door. "Fresh air will do you good."

Jack nodded, knowing Darin was right but also knowing he couldn't afford to lose it now.

At the end of the day shift, around crew change, Jack made a few more phone calls and sought out Olivia in order to remind her he was giving her a lift to EPTC, but he couldn't find her.

He approached Darin. "Have you seen Olivia?"

"Not in about ten minutes," Darin said, wrapping up his cleaning of the grills. "Naem, you seen Olivia? Jack's looking for her."

"I'm supposed to take her to school. Well, to her EMT clinical at EPTC," Jack said to Naem.

"Oh, really? She left with Patrice," Naem said while Darin stepped around them to roll the trash can to the back. "I'm pretty sure Patrice was going to run Olivia by to see about her car real quick."

"Hmm. Maybe she forgot I said I'd give her a ride." Although, Jack didn't think so. The more likely scenario was that she'd rather set herself on fire than have to ride with him…in his Ford.

Jack smiled, thinking about the funny FORD=Found

On Road Dead note she'd left, then the prank boomer-anging back onto her when her car ended up being the one broken down.

He'd actually come to look forward to their car-make sparring. It reminded him of his dad, who was as much a fan of Chevy as Jack was of Ford.

Naem joined them and peered close, with a huge grin of his own. "It's about time."

Jack stiffened. "What?"

Naem smirked. "Thoughts of a woman made you smile."

Jack frowned. "That's ridiculous."

Naem's grin widened "Pretty sure I know who the woman behind your smile is, too."

"Get your boots back to work."

"Dude, I'm off. See? Proof whoever she is has you flustered. Deny it. I dare you."

Jack shook his head. "You don't know what you're talking about."

Naem only laughed louder and smacked Jack hard on the shoulder. "Nice try. But you're not fooling me." The happy-go-lucky Naem walked away whistling and cast a knowing look over his shoulder, along with that mad-deningly perpetual grin.

Jack let out a growl and turned to vacate the premises. And almost plowed into Olivia.

"Oomph!"

Jack grasped her shoulders to keep her from falling. "You all right?"

She let a breath out slowly. "Yeah. Are you in a hurry?"

"No, just…" *Getting away from Naem and his lame suggestion that you make me smile.*

Jack stared at Olivia with the explosive revelation that it was true.

Naem was right.

She *did* make him smile. In fact, he fought it now as he took in her disheveled, slightly irritated-but-not-really look. He was pretty sure that look was a front she forced to hide her shyness.

And maybe even…attraction? Her pupils always dilated and her breath quickened whenever he inadvertently got close.

This close.

Jack realized he'd drifted closer, drawn in by the overpowering depth of her eyes. He wanted to see if he could have that same effect on her again. Delight coursed through him when he realized he could. It met a need he hadn't realized he had until this moment.

He cleared his throat and drifted back slowly, hoping she didn't notice that his sanity had just clocked out and walked off the job.

Her cheeks flushed and she swallowed uncomfortably, proving she had noticed.

Jack scrambled for something to say, to break the awkward, but somehow awesome moment. "Do you still need a ride? Darin said Patrice was taking you to the garage."

"Yeah, I didn't want to have to take you up on that offer but it looks as though I'm going to have to. Patrice has an appointment and my car won't be ready until next week."

Jack wanted to laugh at the look of sheer mock defeat on her face. Yet a nervousness ran in barely detectible currents just beneath that.

Nervousness or anticipation?

He'd be stupid to wish for the latter, but something in him cheered nonetheless.

Darin and Naem waved to the evening-shift crew and passed Jack and Olivia. Darin held out the lapels of the jacket and flannel shirt Jack had given him. "Thanks again for these duds, man. It's great being warm and having something nice to wear for a change."

Olivia peered peculiarly at Darin, his outfit, then at Jack. The admiration in her eyes and smile admittedly bolstered his mood.

"Just talked to Patrice. She is going to the doctor to document her bruises," Olivia said.

"Good. I hope so. That's a step in the right direction."

"Yeah." She grabbed her coat from the employee break room hooks.

"Ready, then?" he asked her, indicating the back door.

Chapter Eight

No. She was far from ready.

"Give me five minutes. I need to go get my dinner for tonight's EMT shift."

"Sure."

"Would you like to come up and wait?"

"Nah. Take your time." Jack's keys jangled as he pulled them out of his pocket. "I'll warm up the Ford."

She didn't miss his teasing smirk and emphasis on *Ford*.

Patrice, standing outside with Darin, giggled and caught up with her. "If I didn't know better, I'd think he was flirting with you."

Jack, Darin and Naem hadn't been letting Patrice out of their sight. At least not while she was at the diner. Olivia was grateful for their protective nature.

"That's preposterous. He just likes to torment me about cars."

"Uh, if I recall correctly, you started that particular war." Patrice wiggled her eyebrows.

"How did you know that?"

"He told me. So, why do you seem so nervous to ride

with him? You have nothing to be scared about. He's the perfect gentleman, I assure you."

"Yeah, I know. Except he's serious about his Fords." Olivia laughed. "I could care less what kind of car I drive just as long as it gets me where I want to go. They all make decent cars. But I must admit it's fun taking Sully's Chevy-over-Ford baton and outrunning Jack with it."

Patrice shook her head. "You and Jack are competitive enough as it is."

The pair climbed the stairs to their apartment above.

After quickly making green smoothies for her and Olivia, Patrice grabbed her makeup pouch and Olivia went to the fridge and got out the sandwich she'd made that morning to save time this evening. Good old ham and cheese, with carrot sticks and chocolate pudding.

"Sully told me Jack trains snipers and heads armies. Add to that the fact that he probably has more guns than a redneck pawnshop, more ammo than Rambo, and when he's not driving Fords he's commanding military maneuvers. It's a little intimidating to say the least."

Dinner and medical bag in hand, Olivia followed Patrice out onto the landing, sipping her smoothie and trying not to cringe that there was probably kale in it. Patrice made the weirdest health shakes sometimes. They were tasty, just as long as Olivia didn't know all the contents.

Patrice turned and gave her a funny look. "But that's not why you're nervous."

Olivia dipped her face, then decided that if she opened up maybe Patrice would, too, about her abuse. She met Patrice's gaze squarely. "Okay, I admit a little intrigue. But it could never work. So it's a dumb daydream. He's just larger than life, handsome and I'm pretty sure he might carry a torch for you, anyway."

Patrice's eyes widened, then she placed her hands on

Olivia's shoulders. "No. He doesn't. Not even a match. Come here." Patrice ushered Olivia back into their apartment. "You have two minutes while Jack warms up his truck. Spill it girl."

She grinned so wide, Olivia smiled, too.

"I'm edgy around him for several reasons. For one, I'm shy and awkward and never know what to say to someone so heroic and formidable, powerful and commanding. He's not exactly the type of guy to talk about the weather."

Patrice laughed. "True."

"The thought of riding with him all week to and from the trauma center is utterly nerve-racking."

"In what ways?" Patrice sipped her smoothie.

"Not only is time spent with him sanding the rougher edges off my initial bad impression of him, his kind acts are turning my irritation with him into intrigue."

To top that, every minute around Jack reminded her of how attracted to him she was beginning to feel. But she didn't feel free to say that to Patrice, on the off chance Jack did like her.

"What are you afraid to tell me?" Patrice said, pegging her.

"What if you weren't with your boyfriend? Would you date Jack if he asked you?"

A weird scraping sound came out of Patrice's throat and she motioned Olivia down the stairs. "No. I'm just going to tell you. Jack and I may be siblings."

Olivia almost stumbled down the last few stairs. At the bottom, she turned and gaped at Patrice. Her serious expression told Olivia she wasn't kidding. "For real?"

She nodded. "We've suspected for years, but because we weren't sure Sully knew, we never said anything. But his mom and my dad apparently cavorted with each other when Sully was overseas and my mom was out of town on her business trips."

Olivia shifted slightly on her feet as the truth sank in. She studied Patrice's bone structure and for once did see a slight resemblance to Jack's. The probability that Patrice was Jack's half sister put Olivia's attraction for Jack in a whole new light.

The more she knew of him and his acts of kindness toward employees off the job, the more that knowledge was wreaking havoc with the well-guarded walls she'd employed around herself.

Things like arranging for a babysitter to use his apartment for the children of employees who have had childcare issues. He'd also given an advance to Darin when his pipes froze and burst in the last storm. Then Jack had shown up to help repair them, plus clean up the mess.

He'd also given evening-shift employees equally kind treatment, including various kinds of off the job assistance when they needed it. There were tons of other things she'd caught wind of that Jack didn't know she knew about.

She imagined there were many kindnesses he'd performed in quiet that she wasn't aware of. In short, he was vested with and invested in his employees. Not just on the job.

They'd all tried to get him to engage in friendship off the clock, but other than help people, he drifted back to being the mysterious hermit he'd become known as.

Olivia was pale when she got into the truck. She glanced at Patrice, who waved at them before getting into her car.

The funny look on Olivia's face as she studied him and Patrice clued Jack in that Patrice had told her they were likely half siblings. She caught Jack studying her, and focused on folding her brown sack tighter.

"I hope she's not going out with her boyfriend again," Jack said, watching Patrice pull out ahead of them.

"Not unless she's planning to break up with him."

"In which case she should have backup with her," Jack said.

Olivia nodded. "Darin and Naem are following her, after she goes to the doctor."

"And the police department, I hope?"

"I couldn't get her to press charges yet. He has her believing he'll get away with it and destroy her in the process."

Jack felt like punching the ceiling. Or wringing Patrice's boyfriend's neck.

A few miles down the road, it became clear Olivia had clammed up. She sat stiffly, breathing evenly, almost purposefully, as though she had to concentrate on even that.

Normally the silence was welcome. But for some reason Jack felt the need to get Olivia talking. "So…" he started as he pulled away from a stoplight at the edge of town that had turned green. "I'm guessing Patrice told you."

Olivia's shoulders loosened. So he was right in that it had been weighing on her whether to say something or not. "Yes. Will you ever be certain?"

"We could have DNA tests. But we're pretty certain now, considering the fact that my dad was overseas when my mom conceived her, and our parents admitted they were involved with each other."

Wanting Olivia to open up about her dyslexia, and also wanting to show her he was beginning to trust her, or at least trying hard to give her the benefit of the doubt, he decided to extend her the courtesy of telling her about his diner plans. He figured now was a good time to discuss them. If she disagreed with him, though, as she often did, it could backfire in his face. But it was a risk he was willing to take. "Since I have your undivided attention for the next ten minutes or so, I thought I'd let you know some more changes I'm instituting at the diner soon."

"*More* changes?" She stiffened and immediately, in his opinion, went on defensive alert.

"I know change is hard for you. Which is why I'm bringing it up now, rather than springing it on you without warning later."

She seemed to relax at that.

"Also, I'd like your input. I'm trying to determine where I can cut diner costs without losing customers."

She nodded as they pulled onto the interstate. "Okay."

"For years, Dad has catered to the locals and given away freebies to some of his buddies. How detrimental do you think it would be to veer away from that for the time being?"

"They're war veterans, Jack. And if you're going to plan to stop catering to them, I think you're making a big mistake," she said thoughtfully, yet still a little guardedly.

"Fair enough. So, what do you suggest?"

"The extended hours, while a sacrifice for workers, was a good idea. Business is picking up. What would you think about doing catering for local businesses or events? There's no one doing that in Eagle Point."

Jack thought about that for a moment. "Who would handle that?"

"Molly, the single mom on evening shift, has always dreamed of running a catering business. But with her triplets and having lost her husband, she's not been able to. I think she'd be perfect for it. She has a fairly new van, and I'm sure she'd be willing to use it to deliver, if you'd reimburse her for gas, mileage, and wear and tear."

"That's not a bad idea. I'll think about it."

Olivia examined him like he was an unknown specimen.

"What?" Jack arched his eyebrow.

"I'm just surprised you didn't argue with me about it." She gave him a smile that nearly stopped his heart.

It actually hurt to see her like that, because he had the feeling she was not going to like the next things he had to say. Not at all.

He was right. By the time he'd finished sharing his thoughts about possibly selling the diner, Olivia looked as though she were about to explode. It was a really good thing they were turning onto the trauma center road.

Jack's cell phone rang. The caller ID said EPTC. His heart leapt into his throat.

Dad.

Speeding up, he asked, "Can you answer that?" since he'd forgotten his Bluetooth.

Olivia took the call and he relaxed when she shrieked and said, "Hurray! When?" She covered the phone. "Sully is awake. He's asking for us."

Us?

Alongside his joy over Dad's improvement, Jack realized with alarm that he liked hearing them referred to as "us." Jack used all his will to shift back to wanting to protect himself.

She beamed and he seethed inside. Why did Dad see them as equal? Made no sense.

Other than the fact that Jack was living on another continent and Olivia was here with Dad.

Maybe it made perfect sense. Still, he didn't like it and didn't fully trust her. Perhaps it was a product of all the betrayal he'd been through in his life, but he felt it was better to err on the side of caution.

After parking, Jack held open the door to EPTC for Olivia.

"I'm texting Patrice, Darin and Naem," Olivia said as they practically sprinted down the halls toward Sully's room. "They'll be so excited Sully's awake."

Jack wanted to tell her not to have everyone converge at the hospital, but in light of the crew's kindness, he fought the urge to be a control freak about it. Really, they cared about his dad, so what was the harm? Other than the fact that it might cut into his time with his father or overwhelm him. Then again, the nursing and medical staff would put a stop to it if they felt there was a risk.

Olivia was so excited that she practically sprinted down the halls ahead of Jack.

Jack gritted his teeth against being the jerk to hold her back and strode to the nurses' station. They waved Jack in. He turned to see Olivia waiting by the desk. He simmered down, realizing she may be holding back to let him have time with his dad first.

"After her doctor's appointment, Patrice is getting the card that she made," Olivia said. "We haven't had a chance to give it to him because he's not been awake to enjoy it. Most of the regular customers and all the employees signed it. Can she bring it by so we can give to Sully?"

Jack remembered it now, the gals taking it around to all the customers that week, and in fact he'd signed it, too. "Fine. But tell her we'll have to make it brief." He headed in and said on his way, "You can see him when I'm done." Then, at the disappointment in her pretty eyes, he softened. "If his doctor says he's up to more than one visitor at a time, I'll come get you."

Clearly he was drawing the line as to who belonged here and who didn't.

The combative but conflicted look on her face gave him the impression she was deeply hurt but trying to be understanding and was grateful for anything she got in terms of being able to visit Sully. Again, Jack wanted to get to the bottom of how this stranger had gotten so close to his dad in Jack's absence. Especially if Dad's faculties had been failing, as the bank officer had gently suggested. Jack still felt there was more to the missing funds than his dad's massive accounting errors. He'd get to the bottom of that, too. Eventually.

So far no one showed signs of being a thief at the diner. But some thieves were very conniving and convincing.

He glanced back at Olivia, expecting to see anger in her eyes. Instead, she smiled, as though happy for him that his dad had woken up.

Which, of course, made Jack felt like an even bigger jerk for walking in without her.

But he really wanted—no, needed—private time with his father. It had been so long.

He stepped around the curtain to see his dad aiming a remote at the TV and clicking back and forth between a home shopping network and a war-history channel as a woman in a blue lab coat gathered some type of machine and a clipboard up in her arms. She looked like a specialist of some kind and said goodbye to his dad as she got ready to leave.

As Jack looked on, he couldn't believe the difference in his father's health, the change for the better.

Jack smiled and tension rolled off his shoulders as relief flooded in at seeing his dad awake and with color returned to his face. And with the typical channels being flipped through. "History and war channels, huh? Some things never change," Jack said, since his dad and the woman hadn't seen him step in yet.

Sully's gaze skipped off the TV and onto Jack. "Jug!" He set the remote down and held out his arms, gathering Jack into a desperate, un-Sully-like hug. "Moy bug jug!"

"Hey, Dad." He hugged his dad as though he was hanging on for dear life. Surprisingly, tears pricked Jack's eyes at the emotion and desperation in his dad's embrace.

"Jug! Moy! Bug!"

The specialist smiled kindly when Jack blinked at the words. "Jack, my boy?" she asked Sully in an effort to translate.

Sully nodded quickly and pointed to her machine then to Jack. "Jug! Moy bug!"

She slid an electronic keyboard tablet toward Sully and he spoke something into it, then poked through the keyboard and showed it to Jack. The screen message said, "Jack, my boy. I've never been so glad to see you, son."

To Jack's surprise, Dad's epic grin and bright-eyed face reflected the emotional pull of the clearly typed message despite the fact that his speech was slurred and garbled. One side of his mouth still drooped slightly, but not as badly as Jack had thought it would. And Dad was using both arms, though one appeared to be a little spastic. That he wasn't paralyzed—only weakened on one side—was a great sign, maybe even a miracle, all things considered.

Thank You, Jack said to the God he'd only spoken to three times in the past year. The first time was the moment his CO had given him the news about his dad. Jack had asked God to spare his dad's life and livelihood. The second time he'd prayed was in the diner the other day, and the third time was just now, in giving thanks to God for answering at least the first prayer even though Jack had lost all faith and hope.

"I'm glad to be here," Jack said, hugging his dad again, tighter this time. They'd never displayed this depth of emotion. And yet he'd always known his dad loved him. He also knew that while Sully was proud of his military service, he worried about him, especially after Jack's unit had come under attack and some were killed by a supposed ally Jack himself had trained.

Being at death's door had really changed Sully.

Sully leaned back into his pillows and muted the TV volume. "Hairs Liver? Taught she's whisker?"

Jack blinked at his dad, then the woman, then the machine as the cursor continued to translate the words that Sully spoke. "Where's Olivia? I thought she was with you?"

"Oh, right. She's out in the hall."

Sully scowled, making Jack feel like the jerk he probably was for not letting Olivia in already. But he really wanted time alone with his dad. That wasn't selfish, was it?

Sully's scowl increased to the point where it became comical.

Jack dipped his head and turned. "I'll just go get her."

When Jack came back around the curtain with Olivia, his dad's arms flew out again, as though expecting a hug. "Liver!" he said.

Olivia shot forward as though to hug Sully, then abruptly braked, head snapping up to peer pensively at Jack. He nodded and extended his hand that it was fine to hug his dad. Free country and all that, right? As they embraced, Jack had to fight the urge to look away.

But, really, he was ashamed of himself and no one else. He should have been here.

As Sully hugged Olivia, her eyes closed with such intense relief, gratitude and joy, Jack couldn't tear his eyes away. She held on and spoke such tender, caring words, Jack knew that she loved his dad like a father and he loved her like a daughter. When she opened her eyes, they glimmered with unshed tears and she swallowed hard while Sully hugged her.

As the hug broke, Olivia darted a glance at Jack, as though scared he'd be upset.

He kept his expression neutral, not wanting his selfish side to have the edge here.

"Hello," Olivia said to the specialist. "You must be Sully's speech pathologist?"

"Yes," the woman answered Olivia. Then to Jack said, "I was about to introduce myself."

Jack nodded. "Nice to meet you. I'm his son."

"Then, this must be your daughter, Sully," the speech pathologist said while looking at Olivia.

Olivia glanced at Jack again. "Actually, no..."

"Like," Sully said that word clearly, to Jack's relief.

"Oh, daughter-in-law, then?" The pathologist looked from Jack to Olivia, as though assuming they were together. Sully immediately started cackling and smacking his knee, probably at the look of sheer horror on Olivia's and Jack's faces.

The speech pathologist straightened, studying the trio. "Oh, since he spoke of the two of you together, I just assumed you were either siblings, married or engaged."

Again, Sully whooped. "Liver and Jug Bug? A troll wash!" He punched a button on his speech tablet.

The speech pathologist leaned over and read the message, and grinned alongside Sully. "This button does audio translation, Sully, remember?"

His eyes brightened and he pushed the button she indicated. "A troll wash." he repeated.

"I truly wish," the machine's robotic voice translated. Then Sully manually typed in something longer. When he was finished, he pushed a button. The speech tablet's robotic voice said, "She'd be a good little mama to my grandbabies and a wonderful wife to my son."

Olivia gasped and her eyes grew so wide that Jack almost joined his dad laughing.

Except that the idea of Olivia marrying him and them parenting a child together was—well, nothing short of absurd. Right?

The speech pathologist studied Olivia, with her edgy, rocker-girl attire, then Jack with his no-nonsense cleancut but hard-boiled military style. "Well, you know what they say about opposites attracting."

Sully appeared to be having tons of fun with this because he typed something else into the little tablet and showed it to the two ladies but not Jack.

And snickered with his new crooked grin.

Whatever he'd typed had the speech lady giggling as they glanced at the tablet, then Jack. Olivia's cheeks turned pink and she darted her gaze quickly away, while tugging sprigs of her spikey hair at the nape of her neck the way she often did around Jack.

Jack tried to look at the speech tablet, feeling a little more irritated than he should that Dad had shut the audio back off. What on earth? He probably didn't want to know what was said, especially since it was clearly about him.

So why was he wasting another second obsessing about it?

He studied Olivia's face for clues. She dipped her head and suddenly found the fringe of her patchwork satchel purse very interesting. No help there.

"I need to get to work," Olivia said, and leaned in to hug Sully once more. "I'll come say 'bye before I leave."

Sully nodded. "Love you, Liver."

That was clear enough.

She leaned in to give him another hug. "Love you, too, Sully. Glad you're getting better."

That Olivia didn't let Sully know that Jack was giving her a ride home indicated that she, too, wasn't keen on Sully getting ideas they were together any more than they had to be.

As Jack watched them, he worried. If Dad had the notion that he and Olivia should be a couple, well, that could be a serious problem. Jack hoped it was just a passing fad with Dad and that he'd forget about it. Sooner rather than later would be good. But the twinkle in Sully's eye as he watched Jack watch Olivia told Jack he wouldn't be forgetting any time soon.

Great.

One more thing to contend with.

The fact that Jack wasn't actually thoroughly opposed to the idea, well, that could be the biggest problem of all.

"I'll be back tomorrow," the speech pathologist said. "Use your tablet."

Sully nodded and she smiled at Jack and Olivia as she left.

A physical therapist entered next to do Sully's evening round of exercises.

"I need to get to work, Sully, and let you get your therapy done so you can rest. See you soon," Olivia said and stepped out without looking at Jack.

"Woc-a-watt." Sully nodded sternly to the door. Jack knew exactly what his dad had said without the help of the tablet. Walk her out.

A few steps down the hall, Jack caught up to Olivia

before she reached the desk. He examined his watch, knowing she had a few minutes yet before she had to report to the trauma bay section. Not that he'd been paying attention to her schedule and whereabouts.

Okay, maybe he had a little.

She peered up, surprise evident that he walked alongside her. "I'm going to get a soda," he hedged. "You want one?"

He thought she'd say no, but she glanced at her bracelet watch and then shrugged. "Sure. I have about five minutes. Soda sounds good."

"So, are you not going to tell me what was on the tablet there at the end?" Jack teased.

"Nope." She straightened as though prepared to battle it out, yet something in her countenance spoke of embarrassment.

"It's natural that my dad's probably going to try to play matchmaker. It's nothing to feel uptight or ridiculed over." Jack truly wanted to ease her obvious discomfort. "I apologize for his orneriness and lack of covertness."

"Look, Jack. Contrary to what you may think, what he said didn't offend me. Any other woman in the world would be glad to have you. You're a great guy."

"Ouch." He laughed. "Any other woman?"

She shook her head, tension leaving her face at how that probably sounded. "I just meant that I know you'd never go out with me, not in a million years. So no apology necessary."

Jack paused and studied her. A million years? Recalling the great regard with which she held his dad, and for all of Jack's run-ins with her, all of which she'd weathered like a trouper, Jack realized that a million years suddenly didn't seem so far away. How he was going to deal with that sudden revelation, he wasn't quite sure.

After buying the sodas, which Olivia tried to protest once she saw that Jack intended to pay for hers, Jack handed her the one she'd chosen. Surprisingly her choice was his favorite beverage, too. They disagreed on so much that it always delighted him to find something they actually agreed on. Such as soda and ice cream flavors. Plus their mutual love for his dad, and saving the diner even if they did have different ideas about how to go about each.

She popped the top of her soft drink and took a swig, and Jack did, as well, while watching her drink. He'd barely swallowed before humor bubbled up from some unknown place.

Her eyes brightened with mirth. "What?"

"Liver?"

She rolled her eyes. "Be quiet, Jug Bug."

Jack laughed. And Olivia joined him. Then, leaning against the vending machine, they both grew serious.

"I'm so glad he's still with us," Olivia whispered. "I'll take Liver any day over never hearing his voice again." Emotion flooded her face as she raised it to peer at Jack's.

The deep emotion in her expression reflected what Jack felt inside and no other words were necessary for understanding their mutual care, gratitude and love for Sully. He didn't know all that this special moment meant, just that it was momentous and pivotal. It built a bond between them that they'd remember years from now—it was that powerful.

It hit him hard and unexpectedly. He felt his throat knot up and a sting surfaced behind his own eyes.

The thought of his dad not being here, Jack couldn't fathom. He knew Olivia shared the sentiment.

He held her gaze and smiled in kind. Then he surprised himself by reaching for her hand, so soft and small in his.

"Yeah. I know just what you mean. I'll take him, ornery and surly and snoopy in our love lives and stubborn, as opposed to not having him here at all." He squeezed her hand.

She smiled, nodding through her vivid smile, then rather reluctantly extracted her hand from his. "I should go."

Jack had only intended his touch to show solidarity and empathy. But when he'd taken her hand, their bond had deepened. He surely hadn't anticipated or expected that.

He wanted to offer to walk her down to the trauma bays. But…why? Maybe he didn't want the moment to end just yet. Confusion swirled in the wake of his inability to reason it out.

These emotions were foreign and they made no sense to him. He didn't much trust the softening shift inside of his heart toward Olivia. Probably it was just the shared emotion over Dad and nothing to be concerned about. After all, what harm could come from bonding over the blessing of a life nearly lost and yet blessedly not?

"See you in four hours?" he asked.

She studied his hands, which were fiddling with his soda, before finally meeting his eyes. "I'll come up to the room when I'm done. That way you're not waiting on me and you can spend as much time with him as possible while he's awake and lucid."

Jack grinned. "Sometimes I can see right through you."

She looked up, eyebrows furrowing.

"That's not always a bad thing, you know. It's okay to admit that you want to see him again before you go."

She held his gaze now. "I wasn't sure how you'd feel about that."

He shrugged. "I'm warming up to the idea. I'm a little slow to come around sometimes. But I usually always come to my senses on something that really matters."

Her eyes widened at his words and she quickly sipped her soda to hide what he perceived as a gaspy little grin.

The mystery of a woman's mind. Jack shook his head and smiled, knowing he'd probably never figure out what she found funny about what he'd just said.

When Jack got back to the room to find his dad resting after therapy, he settled into the chair next to his father's bed. Comforted by the sound of Sully's easy breaths, Jack reached to click the overhead light off, intending to catch a catnap himself. The angle put the tablet in view and Jack found the temptation a little too much to resist.

His eyes scanned the last sentence in the tablet and he didn't know whether to laugh or leave town. The cryptic message Sully had typed and not let Jack see was, "He's a little slow to realize what's best for him at times, but I believe in my heart he'll eventually come around to seeing I'm right."

The tablet screen displayed almost word for word what Jack had said in the vending room to Olivia about himself and coming around to being okay with her closeness with Sully.

Only the tablet version had referred to Dad's notion that Olivia would make a great mom and wife. And Jack agreed wholeheartedly. She would.

Just not for him.

The military, rather than marriage, had long been and still remained Jack's first priority.

That it held less appeal by the day, well, that was just a temporary wrinkle that would be ironed out in time, as Dad's health improved and things with the diner got sorted out.

He just wished he were as sure of that as he wanted to be.

Chapter Nine

❦

"You have to tell him," Patrice told Olivia the next morning as she brought her a washcloth to ease the nausea. Olivia had stayed up so late studying that she was ill. She knew Patrice was right. Jack needed to know the extent of her issues and her special needs. She couldn't keep doing this. She couldn't keep up this crazy schedule. It wasn't working. Not only was she failing, her health was taking a nosedive. How could she take care of others if she couldn't take care of herself?

She'd barely passed her last quiz in her strongest class. Her grades were going down the tubes. If she didn't turn things around this week, she'd be out of the program. "I will. Today."

"In the meantime, you're calling in sick and you're going to stay in bed all day."

Olivia wanted to protest, but in truth, her trembling legs and achy head told her that Patrice was right. She could barely brush her teeth, much less wait on customers on one of the busiest days of the week. Rest was in order.

She had never called in sick and had plenty of sick leave accrued. Jack had not let employees donate their sick days and hours, just their vacation time. So she could take the day off and probably be better off without missing pay. "Okay, but I'll call and tell him."

"How? Your voice is almost gone."

She nodded. Her throat *was* scratchy. "Maybe this is more than fatigue."

Patrice placed her hand on Olivia's forehead. "I think you're right. You're probably coming down with something. Let me tell Jack you won't be in today."

"Fine, but don't tell him anything about my comprehension problem. Pretty sure he knows about my dyslexia, unless he assumed the pamphlet was for school. I'll talk to him about all of it as soon as I'm able to come back to work."

"I'd do it before then. He is getting ready to hire some new people and that would be a good time for him to rearrange your hours to give you a break."

Olivia felt defeat weigh her down. She didn't want special treatment, but the truth was that everyone needed help sometimes. She'd be stupid not to take it if he was willing to work with her. She wanted to be a paramedic—she'd never reach that dream if she didn't get more rest and stay well.

She nodded in resignation to Patrice. "Okay. I'll stay in bed today. I probably need to skip clinical, too." She could always make that up by staying late three or four days next week.

"Don't worry. I'll take care of it."

"Thank you." Olivia tried to stand and grew dizzy. "Can you help me to the restroom?"

Patrice nodded and helped her down the hall. "If you're ill, it may be a few days before you can return to work, class or clinic."

Olivia nodded, knowing she was right but hating it nonetheless. She let Patrice help her from the bathroom back to her bed. She curled back into the covers, never so glad to hug her pillow in all her life. "Thank you," she said as her friend tucked the blankets in around her. That she could sleep in today was a truly beloved bliss she hadn't encountered in over a year. Hopefully proper sleep would chase away this headache. Come to think of it, her body ached, too. All over.

"You've done this for me many times, like that time I had mono." Patrice pulled Olivia's lamp closer to her bed. "I'm glad to help you for a change."

Olivia nodded, trying to stay awake, but the bed had a sedative effect. Or she was just that tired. Patrice came back in with a glass of ice water. She set Olivia's phone on the nightstand and said, "Text me if you need anything. I'll be a quick minute away."

Olivia drifted off knowing Patrice would keep her word. She'd have her phone with her at all times while working double time down at the diner in Olivia's absence. Patrice was a very caring friend. Throat sore, Olivia sent mental prayers up for God to rescue Patrice from the toxic relationship she was in if her boyfriend was never going to change for the better. God would know.

At least Patrice was seeing a counselor and spending less time with Frankie.

Olivia swallowed the two Tylenol tablets Patrice had set near the water and snuggled deeper into the comfort of her bed and fell into a fitful sleep.

What felt like a couple hours later she heard voices. Male and female. Ugh. Had Patrice brought her boyfriend here? Olivia hoped not. The man spoke again. Something about leaving it in the fridge.

Wait. That voice. Not Frankie's. Jack's. What was he doing here?

Olivia wondered if Sully was okay today. What if she'd had a virus brewing days before and made him sick? She summoned the strength to reach for her phone and texted Patrice. Is that Jack I hear?

Yes.

Sully ok?

Yep. U decent?

Yes, why?

Jack wonders if U R up 4 company?

"Really? Weird," Olivia said, realizing how gravelly her voice sounded.

She texted back, Um, well, I'm sure I'm sick, and not just tired.

He says he'll take his chances, Patrice texted back a moment later.

Jack's words via Patrice's text sent a warm fuzzy feeling through Olivia.

There was a knock, then his handsome face appeared. She really must be delirious because he looked a thousand times better today than every other day. And he was pretty handsome as it was.

"Hey, kiddo. I hear you're under the weather."

Kiddo? Olivia bristled at that. He was only three or four years older than she.

She sneezed into a tissue then put it into an old popcorn bucket and sanitized her hands. "Yeah. A little cold and just really tired."

"Mind if I come in for a bit?"

"I don't want to get you sick. I'm worried I exposed your dad to illness. Though I felt well yesterday."

"He's fine." Jack stepped in, despite her concern of being contagious. She tried to sit up.

"No, stay in bed. I just wanted to let you know there's some chicken soup in the fridge for when you feel up to eating it."

Surprise went through her. "Chicken soup. Like from a can?"

Jack eased onto the footstool next to her bed and smiled. "No, like chicken soup made from scratch for an ill employee." He slid a box of tissues closer when she reached for it.

She'd have rather he called her a friend than an employee but he'd drawn that line.

"Okay, *friend*, then," Jack said with a strange smile.

She blinked. "Did I say that out loud?"

Concern and humor filled Jack's eyes. "About wanting to be called a friend? Yep." He dipped a cloth in the cool bowl of ice water Patrice must have brought in at some point. He wrung it out and dabbed it across Olivia's forehead.

"That feels good. Even though I'm freezing."

"Your skin feels hot." He frowned. "You look glassy-eyed and feverish."

"I'm probably just dehydrated. Chicken soup sounds good, actually." She did feel hungry. That was positive, right?

"It's still warm. Would you like a cup now?"

"Sure." She started to pull the covers off to swing her legs over the side of the bed when Jack's hand rested on her shoulder.

"I'll get it. You stay here."

Olivia obeyed simply because the thought of moving

seemed impossible right now. Her legs felt like lead and her head as if someone was smashing bricks inside of it. Her muscles ached all over and her throat felt as though someone had taken a torch to it. This definitely was more than lack of sleep and simple fatigue.

When Jack returned a moment later, he had the soup on a tray with a diner napkin, salt and pepper, some crackers on a saucer and a steaming cup of what smelled like peppermint tea.

Her stomach growled, but her throat protested the first swallow. "Ow."

"Too hot?"

"No. Throat hurts." She sipped more broth, not trusting herself to be able to swallow anything solid. She truly felt lousy. "This is really good." The soup's flavor was amazing. The salty warmth soothed her throat. Maybe she should gargle salt water. She opted for another sip of broth. "So good," she said. Some dribbled down her chin because of the angle at which she drank, plus only half sitting up.

Jack reached over and dabbed the moisture off with the napkin. He brushed the soft cotton across the curve of her lip, then to the side where she'd missed a spot. His gaze followed his motions, moving from her chin to her mouth and up to her eyes, where it settled. His smile deepened. This close, she could see the tiny whiskers in his dimples that his razor missed, and the scar on the edge of his manly chin.

"You smell good." Somewhere in the rational part of her mind, Olivia knew she'd never have spoken such a thing if her mind wasn't woozy. Somehow his cologne made breathing easier. Her gaze settled back on his chin scar, which stretched with his killer smile.

She remembered Sully saying he'd been hit by a flying baseball bat in sixth grade and needed seven stitches there. The worst part was that the girl who'd thrown the bat during an unexpected home-run hit was a girl Jack had had a crush on forever.

"Women are trouble," she murmured.

"Tell me about it," Jack said, his smile deepening as he rubbed a thumb across his scar. Almost as though he knew her mind was replaying Sully's story.

Weird how they could slip into unspoken sync one second and be at odds the next.

That she remembered nearly every one of Sully's daily stories about Jack was a tribute to the strong memory God had blessed her with. Without it, she'd never pass EMT school. Not with her comprehension problem and her reading disorder.

Maybe those daily stories of Jack also accounted for the tenderness she felt for him right now, in this dim, intimate setting where the lamp illuminated the pleasant facets of his face. The man could be a top-notch movie star. His features were so striking that it was hard not to feel all awkward and befuddled around him. Except, right now, she felt comforted and completely comfortable and safe in his protective, caring presence.

Their eyes met and held with a powerful array of emotions, ones she couldn't even begin to decipher just yet. She needed a distraction so she said, "Soup was superb." She'd never tried it at the diner. She saved soup eating for when she was sick, which was hardly ever.

Smiling, Jack said, "I do run a diner in my spare time you know. The recipe is Dad's. Although I confess to having help from Darin. And Naem sent this homemade Israeli pita bread to dip in it." Jack unwrapped a foil packet at the edge of her tray.

"Oh, you all love me."

Jack startled at that. Her throat hurt too much to explain she'd meant it in a comradely sense. "Sure you don't need to see a doctor? Maybe get a strep or flu screen?" he asked.

"If I feel worse in a couple hours, I will."

Jack picked up a thermometer that Patrice must have set by Olivia's bedside. Although Olivia didn't remember when. She must've been drifting in and out of sleep all day.

Jack removed the lid from the thermometer, put a probe cover on and swept a thick lock of Olivia's hair away from her ear. He inserted the thermometer into her ear and smiled. "Tympanic is more accurate to the core body temperature," he told her.

The thermometer beeped and his brow furrowed at the reading. He met Olivia's eyes. "102.5. You need to see a doctor, Liver."

She laughed at that inside joke, glad it was a way they could cope with the devastating effects of Sully's stroke, but then the laughter made her start coughing. She quickly faced away from Jack and tried to cover her mouth with a tissue. Maybe he shouldn't have been seated so close. She dearly hoped Jack didn't get her germs.

He didn't seem concerned, although he did rise to use her sink to wash his hands. He also pulled out his cell phone and made a call while at the sink. Olivia took a second to rest her itchy eyes. What seemed only a moment later, a second voice had joined Jack's.

Jolting awake, Olivia bolted up. Or tried to. Dizziness accosted her head. It felt like a cinder block. She promptly fell back to the pillow. She blinked at the man's name tag. Dr. Riviera from Refuge Memorial Hospital. That's who Jack must've called by the sink. How long ago had that been? By the level of light peeking in past her blinds, it looked to be late in the day now.

Dr. Riviera nodded to Jack. "I see what you mean."

"What?" she asked in a terribly frail voice. She was sweating bullets and freezing now.

"Olivia, try to blow your nose but hold it closed."

She eyed him oddly, then realized she'd seen this test. "Okay." The doctor did a nose swab, then a throat culture.

"Jack said your symptoms came on pretty suddenly?" the doctor asked. Olivia nodded, simply because her throat felt like it was on fire now.

Who did house calls nowadays, anyway? She was glad for this doctor, and grateful to Jack for getting him here. She tried to convey that with her eyes. Jack nodded, his smile strong but tender.

After several minutes, the doctor said, "Your strep screen is negative but you are positive for influenza B."

"Ugh. I can't be sick. I have two tests this week that I can't miss." She was already behind because of the tests she'd failed and had had to make up, barely passing each.

The doctor smiled but shook his head. "No school or work for the rest of the week."

What? No. "That's four whole days."

"Yes. Any less and I fear you'll end up hospitalized, young lady. School can be made up. Rest, meds and fluids are in order." To Jack he said, "I'll call in some Tamiflu for you to pick up. Have her start taking it immediately." The doctor wrote something down on paper. "Here are the other instructions for her care." He looked abruptly up at Jack. "Also, if you've had mouth-to-mouth contact with her, or anything of that nature, we should probably treat you, as well."

"What?" Jack's eyes widened. "Mouth to mouth—"

"As in kissing, Jack. Not CPR." Dr. Riviera leveled him with a humorous look. "Nice try for density, man."

Jack blinked, then blushed as red as the plastic Solo cup Olivia's Sprite was in.

She wanted to giggle at the confounded look on Jack's face and, in fact, nearly did.

She pressed her face into her pillow to keep it in, because if she laughed she'd start coughing again, and coughing really hurt her throat.

"Yeah, so I'll just go get that Tamiflu," Jack said stiffly and went to wash his hands.

The doctor set some other medications next to Olivia. Then he said to Jack, "Let me know if you need me to call in two orders of Tamiflu."

"I do not," Jack said firmly, and sent the doctor a stern look.

Olivia had missed that endearing no-nonsense scowl.

Dr. Riviera studied Olivia to see if she'd refute Jack's denial. "No kissing?"

Olivia shook her head and tried not to start giggling again. "No, but he was in the path of a rogue cough earlier," she whispered to the doctor.

"Okay, so, for the close proximity let's go ahead and start Jack on Tamiflu, too."

Jack whirled. "Beg your pardon?"

"Just a precaution, Jack," the doctor said.

Jack sent Olivia a surly look, as if maybe he knew she'd ratted him out over the cough.

She raised her chin, daring him to argue with the doctor.

He shook his head and closed the door a little harder than necessary upon exit.

Olivia rasped out a laugh. "He thinks you don't believe him."

"Or he thinks you told me he kissed you." Dr. Riviera

grinned. "Although I will say you two looked pretty cozy when I walked in."

"Pretty sure that, since I don't remember you walking in, I was comatose."

"Strike that, then. Jack seems worried about you. He was glued to your side when I walked in."

Olivia felt flustered. They hadn't been that close. Had they? "Either way, I think you sufficiently embarrassed him," Olivia said.

"We're old military buddies. Believe me, it wouldn't hurt the guy to loosen up and laugh again." Dr. Riviera faced Olivia. "We work out together and give each other grief on a regular basis. Trust me, I owed him one in terms of a good razzing. I'm just glad you played along."

She smiled and looked at all the stuff he'd brought. She'd never had the flu, to her knowledge. Of course, her parents rarely, if ever, took her to the doctor when she was ill. She couldn't recall a time when they'd gotten her help when she'd needed it, which was why her dyslexia wasn't discovered until her senior year in high school. The school guidance counselor, who also happened to be a part-time EMT, picked up on it while helping Olivia work through grade struggles.

She'd been a lifesaving friend and a mentor of sorts to Olivia, especially through family trauma and drama. Then she'd perished in a car crash later that year. Olivia had been devastated, and determined then to become an EMT and eventually a paramedic, which had also been her counselor's dream. Olivia's heart ached remembering the kindness, the lasting impact and the restorative feeling of an adult finally believing in her and helping her.

Dr. Riviera's voice cut into the hard memory. "Jack has my number. Have him call me if you feel worse."

"I will if he's here."

"He gave me his word he's taking care of you. That is the only reason I'm not making you go to the hospital. I'd prefer you not be exposed to all the bacteria there, anyway."

Olivia was shocked. Had Jack offered to do that? Or had the doctor asked him?

"If you get to where you can't drink or keep fluids in, he needs to bring you to the ER. Or if your fever rises above 103. Or if you become short of breath or feel worse in any way whatsoever."

She nodded, knowing all of that and glad for the recall, even amid illness. "Thank you."

Patrice poked her head in. "Oh, excuse me. I didn't know you were still here."

"Just leaving, actually." He winked good-naturedly at Olivia. "Since Patrice has been exposed, we're treating her with Tamiflu, as well."

So his kissing question was all just a ploy to give Jack a hard time. She grinned, really liking this doctor. He said to Patrice, "Jack went to the pharmacy to get the meds I called in."

"Oh, good. I'll sit with her until he gets back."

Dr. Riviera handed Patrice a mask to put on, then explained what all of the items that he'd brought were for. Olivia listened as best she could with the fog in her brain. Patrice walked the doctor to the door, then rapidly returned to Olivia's bedside.

"You look so ill." Patrice dabbed Olivia's brow with a cloth. "Can I get you anything?"

"Actually, can you help me take a shower? I'd feel better." She probably smelled like a pond, she'd perspired so much.

Plus, Jack was coming back and she knew she looked a wreck.

"Are you sure you're up for that?"

"Maybe if we put that plastic chair in there, I could just sit under the water for a bit. I think the water mist would break up my cough, too."

"Okay, sure." Patrice grabbed towels, fresh pajamas and turned on the water before helping Olivia in. After a brief shower, she dressed and let Patrice help her back toward the bed.

"Dizzy?"

"A little." Her legs were wobbly and profoundly weak by the time she made it back to bed. She fought tears. "What if my instructors don't let me make up the week's tests?"

"They will. We'll pray they do."

Olivia nodded and leaned on her friend as she pulled the fresh covers back. "Clean sheets and blankets. You made my bed?"

"With help. Jack came back before you got out of the bathroom and he helped change your linens."

"How embarrassing."

"He even put peppermints on your pillowcases. He seemed glad to have something to do. He's a problem solver. So putting him to work when he feels helpless is a good thing."

"The dangerous and highly decorated commander Jack Sullenberger, helpless? What's he feel helpless about?"

Patrice almost said something, then paused. She studied Olivia, then her closed door and leaned in. "He's really worried about you, Olivia. Seeing you this ill has really thrown him off-kilter. Just between me and you—I think he *really* cares."

"Yeah, I've seen that side of him lately. The soft, mushy side he tries to hide."

Patrice helped pull the covers up around Olivia and

then rested hands on her shoulders. "No, sweet naive one. I meant that I think he really cares…about you."

Whoa.

Olivia let her gaze skip across the bedside table to the thermometer. "Check your temp. I think you're the one in a delirium-drenched fever now."

Patrice laughed. "Say what you will. I've known Jack for a long time. I've never seen him this way toward anyone." She brushed damp but freshly shampooed hair from Olivia's eyes. "No, mark my words. There is something there. Definitely not my imagination, Olivia."

While Olivia grappled with Patrice's words, Patrice took great care to rearrange and meticulously straighten the items the doctor had left. "There. Much better and brighter."

"Aw. You put them into a flower shape." Olivia smiled. Her nightstand now looked like a flu treatment garden. "You are such an artist at heart. You need to pursue design school, Patrice."

She nodded. "Yeah, once I take care of—other things, maybe I will."

"Promise?" Olivia shifted in bed to sit straighter but couldn't get high enough for her liking.

Patrice helped Olivia lean forward, then stuffed another pillow behind her. "I promise that, if you promise me something in return."

Olivia settled back into the pillows and took the Tamiflu capsule Patrice gave her. "Promise what?"

She leaned in and whispered, "To give Jack a chance if I'm right."

Gulp.

Olivia blinked at Patrice but the sound of a door opening and closing followed by Jack's baritone voice threading down the hallway prohibited them from further discussing it. Which was probably best. With her not feeling up to par, the idea held more appeal than it probably would have if she were in her right mind.

Once the flu fled and Olivia was well and caught up on rest, the notion of kissing Jack—and of pondering a romantic relationship with him—would stop running on a constant loop in her mind. She hoped.

Her defenses were simply down.

"He's probably just stressed about me being sick because we're one server down at the diner. All this is just a temporary glitch. You'll see."

Patrice smirked and handed Olivia a glass of water. The knowing glint in her eyes, as well as the fact that Patrice didn't feel inclined to defend her claim, left Olivia wondering. Was Patrice right? And, if so, what would that mean? It wasn't like Olivia could do something about it. Too many roadblocks. Or, in Jack's case, roadside bombs.

The thought of him returning to war zones frightened her like never before.

Sully was making fabulous progress, for which she was grateful. But that also meant that Jack would likely return to duty soon. Once he was on the other side of the world again, she'd be a million miles away from his heart. Then any seed of sweet surrender that Sully's stroke had planted between them would surely wither before it even had the chance to grow.

"Olivia?" Jack whispered so as not to startle the sleeping beauty. He wasn't used to seeing her without all of her dark makeup and rock concert jewelry. Her face was striking, her eyes more stunning than usual.

And staring right into his in the next blink.

"Hey, Liver." He used their special endearment, glad

to see it still elicited an instant smile. "I hated to wake you but we're already late on your next dose of Tamiflu."

"No, Patrice just gave me one," Olivia said, counting the pills that were left. She'd had three?

"That was last night. I let you sleep as long as I could," he said softly as she stretched and stirred.

Her arm emerged from under the blanket, to reach for the water, he thought. But instead, she rested her hand on his. And patted. And patted. And patted. He dipped his head, trying not to snicker. "You can be so nice," she murmured in a half daze.

He chuckled. "And that surprises you?"

She turned over, more awake now. "Mmm, yeah, kinda." She struggled to sit up.

Jack leaned over to help her by sliding his arm behind her back and lifting her higher in the bed and then to a sitting position. "Better?"

She nodded, but averted her eyes.

It could be the fact that they were practically nose to nose was making her nervous.

"You shouldn't be this close."

"You've gone over twenty-four hours without a fever and had several doses of Tamiflu. I doubt you're contagious anymore." He handed her a tube of lip balm. "Here. Your lips are chapped."

She met his gaze. When her eyes dropped to his mouth then away, he realized how intimately he was holding her. He eased her shoulders back onto her pillows and put space between them. They reached for her water at the same time, and their hands connected.

She quickly pulled hers back. "Sorry."

He smiled. "What are you afraid of, Olivia?" His voice sounded thick to his own ears. He'd meant the question in a teasing sense, sort of like kids on an elementary school playground attempting to avoid cooties.

But when her eyes met his, they were more telling than she probably realized. The attraction flared, and this time his gaze dropped to her mouth before returning to her eyes.

He knew exactly what she was afraid of.

This attraction had started out a slow simmer on day one and now, after three days of his being at her side, had boiled over. There wasn't a lid in sight that could stop it.

To deny it would be dumb. To acknowledge it aloud, not much better. Ignoring it altogether seemed the safest option. So that's what he did. Or tried to.

Once she got better, this weirdness would go away. Yet the thought of no longer taking care of her made him sad in ways he didn't know how to comprehend or process.

"Tamiflu?" she said, breaking him out of his mixed-up thoughts.

"Yeah." He reached for the dose, peeled the paper back and slid the capsule into her hand. She popped it into her mouth with more energy than he'd seen her have in days, then swigged several sips of water as he held the cup. Afterward, she let out a long breath without coughing.

"Feeling better?"

She nodded. "Much."

He grinned at the sprigs of bed head hair sticking up at the crown of her head. He dipped his chin so she wouldn't notice. He wasn't making fun of her whatsoever. He found the fresh-mussed look adorable.

"I need to talk to you about something," she said, her voice a little hoarse.

He handed her the cup again and she took another few sips. Her appetite seemed better, too. He was glad she was on the mend. Dad had been asking about her daily.

Jack would be glad to see the worry lines ease from the nondroopy side of dad's face. He really loved Olivia as though she was his own daughter.

And he'd been hinting nonstop about how Jack and Olivia would make a great team.

Jack hated to discourage his dad and so he'd just sat quietly, pretending to consider it.

Funny thing, though. After about three days, Jack realized that at some point he'd actually started listening, *really* listening to the stories Sully told about Olivia through the tablet. It had picked up on Dad's voice tone, patterns, cadence and all that to be accurate. Stories Jack was sure Sully picked because they'd put her in a good light in Jack's mind. And they had.

"So, did you want to talk now?" Jack set her water down and opened the package of saltine crackers next to her bed, hoping she could take solid food now. She'd barely been able to keep down clear liquids. His soup had remained her favorite, which didn't hurt his ego.

She drew a deep breath and her sigh hitched. He thought at first that she was going to cough, but then she wrung her hands together and he realized she was just nervous.

Whatever she had to say was going to be very hard for her.

Jack set the crackers aside and leaned forward. "Olivia?"

She raised her gaze. "I hate to admit this, but it's not fair to you if I don't."

He nodded. "Go on."

She tried to clear her throat. He handed her the water. After a small sip, she used a napkin to swipe her mouth then settled her gaze to his. "As you know, probably from the pamphlet I left, that I have dyslexia. But I also have another pretty severe learning disability in addition to that."

He nodded. He'd figured the part about the dyslexia.

"The learning disability is a comprehension problem that is exacerbated when I don't get enough sleep."

Jack dipped his head. "The schedule." He felt terrible. Not only had his earlier hours caused her to fail a number of quizzes, lessons and tests in EMT school, according to Patrice, it had put her health at risk by making her more susceptible to the flu that had taken her down for days. "I'm sorry."

"It's not your fault. I should have told you up front, when you asked in the beginning."

"I'm happy to cater to your needs. I want to see you get through school. I know how important it is to you."

She nodded. "It is. And I appreciate it. But it's also important to me not to leave the diner or your dad, my coworkers—or you for that matter—in the lurch."

"I appreciate that. So let's come up with a compromise."

Over the next half hour, Jack and Olivia discussed options for her. He let her know that he'd hired a hostess who could cover her server spot for the few early hours in the morning, so she could come in at nine instead of five.

"Four more hours of sleep sounds heavenly," Olivia said. "But will the new worker be okay with coming in at five in the morning?"

"She prefers to come in before dawn and leave at one. I'll stagger your shift so you can come in later and leave earlier, if need be, on days you need to study."

"Can you afford to hire people to cover this, Jack? Be honest."

"I'll make it work one way or another."

She didn't look as if she cared much for his answer,

but one step at a time. He knew she'd probably fret over her lost pay, but he had a way around that, too.

He'd decided to make her the shift manager on days. That promotion came with a raise. He'd wait to tell her until she returned to work, though. For now, she had enough on her plate.

"You still look very troubled."

She nodded. "My instructor called while you went to visit your dad. They can't push my makeup test back. They said I can take it by computer, but the program director wouldn't give me a break on the timeline." Fear filled her eyes that she couldn't quite blink away.

"When do you have to take it?" Jack asked.

"Monday." She peered over at her EMT books. "Today's Friday. I've felt too lousy to study. I don't think I can learn it in three days."

"Would it help if I read it to you and maybe quizzed you on it?"

"You've already done so mu—"

"No buts. If it'll help you, just say yes." He tried to say it sternly, but his voice must not have held the usual edge because she smiled.

"If you're sure?"

"I want to see you succeed, Olivia. I know you can do this." He reached for her books. "Tell me where to begin."

"Page seventy-seven. Thank you, Jack. I never thought I'd be able to say this to you because of my background and our history of not always seeing eye to eye. But it feels comforting to have someone strong and confident in my corner."

He returned her smile, surprised at the powerful impact her words had on him as well as the sincerity with which she spoke them.

"Maybe it's good, you know?" He flipped open her chapter.

"What's that?"

"You're always so strong. You're one of the toughest people I know, Liver. I think it's good that you're finally letting yourself lean on someone else's strength, if even for a day."

She grinned. "Or two. Those are monster big chapters, Mr. Ford-loving Commander."

He grinned and cracked open her workbook, knowing in his heart that if she kept smiling at him that way and giving him such sweet compliments with that look of great respect, he'd be tempted to spend the rest of his life living up to her words.

It was just too bad that their lives were on two different paths.

He should be grateful that their lives had intersected at all. But, instead, he felt sad.

He'd just received word that, as soon as Sully was recovered enough for Jack to return to duty, he was being reassigned to Syria.

He looked at Olivia and felt a twinge of sorrow over the fact that in a matter of weeks they'd be having none of these ribbing but real conversations. She'd be in one country and he in another. So the fact that she clearly had a place in his heart was something he was better off not mentioning to her.

And the ache he was beginning to feel when he wasn't with her? He would have to man up and cope with it, and hope it would fade completely away.

For the first time in a long time, Jack didn't look forward to his future overseas.

And, looking into Olivia's eyes as he began to read her chapters to her, he knew for certain that the ache inside had absolutely nothing to do with switching assignments from Afghanistan. He'd always wanted to return to Syria. But the idea of not hearing her voice or seeing the expressive way her mouth moved and the way her eyes shone when he spoke? Yeah. He'd miss her.

As he read and watched her soak in the material, he wondered…

He thought of Syria and how much he'd loved serving there.

He thought of Olivia and how it had felt to take care of her.

Life here, with Olivia and Dad…or military life.

Which one would he miss more?

That Jack could no longer readily answer that threw up a huge red flag.

These sorts of thoughts would be the death of his dream of retiring military after he'd brought retribution and justice to the traitor who'd taken the lives of his men as well as the lives of innocent civilians who'd harbored them.

No, the new intel said the military mole had slipped into Syria and his superiors wanted to know if Jack wanted first dibs to run point and send a team in to find the foe who'd feigned allegiance. If Jack didn't see to the justice of senseless loss, no one would.

And that would haunt him for the rest of his life. More so than leaving Olivia and his Dad here, not knowing if he'd come back to this country alive.

He had to go.

Which meant he had to let go.

Chapter Ten

"Are you home for good, I hope?" the voice asked after Sully had spoken the semigarbled sentence into his tablet while pressing a piece into a jigsaw puzzle he, Olivia and Jack worked on. It amazed Jack how accurately the machine translated words. He was thankful Dad was showing signs of improvement after only a few weeks of rehab. And yet Sully still faced major challenges.

Jack had his own challenge to face, in that he had no idea how to answer Dad's question. He could feel Olivia's curious eyes on him as well as the weight of his dad's hope. The decision wasn't going to be easy.

To stay or go?

His dream had always been to return. But these days, the dream didn't squeeze on his heart as hard as seeing Dad each day. Regardless, he owed his dad an answer.

Jack stalled by pretending to study the red saddle pattern atop a palomino of the Western-themed puzzle.

The hope in his dad's face was nearly too much to take. It made Jack want to tell his dad yes, that he was home from war for good. Except that might not be the truth. Nor did he want to tell his dad that it depended on how well he recovered from the stroke because that could affect his progress.

So he simply smiled, held up a puzzle piece and said, "We'll see. But chances are, I can make that happen if need be." He pressed a piece into the horse's mane.

There. Put the outcome on the military. And that was partly true. Although Jack knew he could probably retire with one phone call tomorrow. It was just a matter of whether he wanted to. He'd wanted to get twenty years in for as long as he could remember. He'd trained and prepared for it forever.

That said, he'd settle for fifteen good years at this point. Anything to reconcile the wrong, and erase the mistake of lives lost because he'd trusted someone who didn't deserve it. Jack's hand tightened on the puzzle box as he studied the cowgirl whose vivid eyes reminded him of the woman staring across the table at him.

Olivia's gaze tracked from Jack to Sully and back. Then she rose. "Thank you for inviting me to work on the puzzle with you, Sully. My break is over, so I should get back to work."

Sully looked disappointed to see her go, but he also looked proud of her. He blew her a fatherly kiss and Olivia gathered her medical bag and went on her way. "'Bye, guys."

Jack rose to walk her to the door. Once there, Olivia said quietly, "I know it's a tough decision, whether to return to deployment. I'll be praying for you, Jack."

He nodded, touched by her words. Faith issues were touchy for him, and she was so strong in hers. She never preached, just befriended, which helped.

She paused as though considering her next words. "For what it's worth, I hope you stay."

For a whisper, the words hit him like a neutron bomb.

Before he could read her face, she turned and quickly went down the hall.

Did she hope he stayed for Sully? Was that it?

As he made his way back to the table, Jack suddenly didn't know if even one more year serving with distinction abroad amid danger would be worth the time he'd lose here. No matter what difference he'd make.

Sully's hand shook as he pressed a piece next to the one Jack had just put in. Jack would have felt better about his answer if it weren't Dad's strong hand trembling.

"I sure hate to see you go back over there." Sully's tongue worked, whether from emotion or concentration, Jack wasn't sure. He was glad to see Dad try to use his stroke-affected hand now as he fiddled with the voice tablet. "Lots of people around here'll miss you. But no matter what you do, you know I'm proud of you."

It was a rare glimpse of vulnerability to see his dad this way. Just then, Sully swiped the puzzle piece from Jack's hand and put it into its proper spot. He smirked and said, "Amateur."

Jack laughed, knowing it was moments like this that made the best memories. Only he didn't want just memories with Dad, but more of the moments.

In fact, the thought of missing moments with Dad cast an anxiety over Jack that he was pretty sure he'd never encountered before.

There'd be other people Jack would miss, too, goodbyes he was growing to dread more by the day. People like Darin and Naem, who were becoming his trusted friends, despite how thickly Jack had drawn lines against it. Patrice, essentially his only sister, and even Perry, for all of his attitude, was starting to grow on Jack. Not that he'd admit it to any of the diner crew. Not yet, anyway. None of them even knew, as far as Jack knew, that he was hanging out with Perry in a big brother sense. He'd managed to talk the kid into checking himself into rehab—a big step.

But the one person Jack would miss more than anyone else was Olivia.

How she'd climbed all his fortified fences and leaped over all those walls he had no idea.

The worst part was, he didn't even think she knew.

Somehow he'd come to really care about her. And not in the same brotherly way he cared about Patrice. No, his care for Olivia was exactly the kind that could justify the two separate prescriptions of Tamiflu if he hadn't held himself in check until she completely got better. Her smile had become more contagious than the flu. Caring for her had created a bond he was ill prepared for.

The truth was, the moment Riviera teased him about kissing her was the moment Jack realized desire had already been simmering under the surface. Would she kiss him back…or slap him? Jack grinned at either scenario because whichever way it went, it would be fun and fiery.

The physical therapist arrived, announcing it was time for Sully to walk. After a trip a little farther up the hall than yesterday, Jack and the nurse helped Dad back to his room. Dad's last few steps were weak and precarious. But Sully was determined.

Jack was glad doctors had opted to leave Sully at EPTC for the time being, since they had the room and staff and knew it would enable Jack's ease in visiting.

Jack was also glad to see him progressing from the walker to the cane. "He's doing better with that new dancing partner than I thought he would."

Sully grinned at Jack's referencing his cane and his dancing partner. "Yeah, Olivia even named her."

"She did, did she?"

"Yeah, Loopin' Lucy because they always make me

walk an extra lap with it. Also, I always loved the name Lucy. Lucille Ball was my favorite star."

"I remember that show," the PT said. "Now I'm dating myself." She grinned at Sully, then turned to Jack. "So, what about your dancing partner? I didn't catch her name?"

"Uh, who, what?"

"The petite pretty young lady who looks like an eighties songstress who stepped off a Joan Jett record. The one who looks like a rock star, but looks at *you* like you're her rock star."

"Who, me?"

"Yes, when you're not looking. She's checking you out."

Sully started snickering. And nodding his head. The traitor.

"Don't you have your next patient to torture?" Jack said to the physical therapist and nodded to her clipboard full of rooms to visit.

She let out a hearty chuckle. "Yeah, but none are as easy to tease as you."

Sully nodded and spoke into the tablet, which robotically translated, "It's true."

"At least she was teasing and not serious," Jack said to Sully while helping him settle in the recliner next to the bed.

She dipped her head around the corner while washing her hands. "FYI, just because I teased you about her checking you out, doesn't mean it's not true. I think there's a spark there. Don't you, Sully?"

"Yowza good spock dare. Bean team. Liver and moy bug Jack, yeah!"

Yeah, there's a good spark there, between Olivia and my boy Jack, yeah!

Jack didn't need the tablet to understand that one.

Jack issued his dad a stern look. "I thought I'd confiscated all of Cupid's arrows in here, old man. Enough with the romance fluff. You know that's not on my radar."

Sully's face fell a little. So Jack took the edge off his words by winking at his dad.

Sully scowled and his face almost looked normal. Then he garbled into the audio machine, "Maybe it would be on your radar if you weren't so stone-face stubborn."

Jack busted out laughing, mostly because his dad was exactly right.

Puzzle finished, Jack powered his laptop on to show Dad how he was changing from paper schedules to computerized. He'd shown it to Olivia and she'd actually liked it, but then told him it would go over with Sully like a lead balloon. Time to test her theory.

"When this thing updates the downloads, I want to show you something cool. Something I think will make our lives easier with scheduling."

He didn't want his father to think he meant all of Dad's doctor visits, stroke rehab and various therapy appointments. So he added, "Diner staff and maintenance scheduling. To make things at the diner run more smoothly."

Sully scratched his temple. Spoke something into the tablet which translated, "Sounds fishy. Don't think I care for computers much. Is the diner okay? What's going on there?"

Jack could tell that his dad was anxious about it because his heart rate and blood pressure spiked. He wanted to calm and reassure him. "Things are going fine. Great, actually."

"You never were a good fibber," the robotic voice accused. Sully scowled, but a twinkle of a grin rested behind his bright blue eyes. He spoke into the translator again, "Son, now really tell me what's going on or you know I'll worry. I've been asking for a week."

This morning's meeting with all of Dad's caregivers had resulted in a combined game plan for restoring Sully to health. Everyone present was in agreement that Sully would probably have less stress if he felt as though he still had his hand on the reins of the diner, at least on a few important things.

Jack had brainstormed what those things could be and the doctors had agreed that the decisions he could let Sully make would benefit Sully and buoy his dignity, which he felt had been lost in the stroke and in his inability to run the diner right now.

The doctors also agreed that not letting Sully have any diner say or input was putting him at risk for another stroke and a setback in his long-term outlook and eventual rehabilitation.

"We're in transition with some things, but the changes are good." Maybe Dad would have insight into who'd be a good crew leader for each of the two shifts. Plus, if Jack let Sully make those kinds of decisions, he'd still feel like he had control over the diner and his life. That would be therapeutic and beneficial. The last thing Jack wanted was for his dad to feel useless. "Actually, Dad, I'd love your opinion on a few things."

Sully grinned. "Shoot," the tablet said.

"What would you think about having crew leaders, for times you or I have to leave the diner?" *If* Dad ever was able to return.

"Crew leaders." Sully appeared to chew on that. Then his mouth flattened. "Dumbest thing I ever heard."

Well, Olivia was right again. Scratch the crew leader idea.

"I'd like to hire new people and have current crew

members train them. Who from each shift do you think would be ideal for that?"

"Evening shift…Miss Molly. Day shift…our Olivia."

"You're sure about that?"

Sully scowled and pushed replay on the tablet translator. "Evening shift… Miss Molly. Day shift…our Olivia," the robotic voice repeated.

That Dad had called her *our Olivia* sent an odd feeling through Jack. Up until now, he'd really thought his dad had just been kidding.

Jack studied his eyes and caught a determined glint not there before. So perhaps not?

To make Molly a crew trainer might prevent her from doing the catering thing, though, as Olivia had suggested. Jack just didn't know how well that would go over.

If the diner did end up pulling out of debt, at that time, he'd revisit Olivia's idea of Molly catering out of Sully's Diner. That would be mutually beneficial, plus bless the town and make a better life for a struggling single mom.

"Molly will be glad for the promotion and raise, but Olivia won't feel worthy of it," Sully said through the speech tablet. "In fact, I can almost guarantee Olivia's going to fight you tooth and nail on it. But hold your ground, son, because I think the leadership would be good for her."

"You don't think the employees will feel pitted against each other if I give Olivia and Molly that distinction?" That had been Olivia's concern with crew leadership.

"Maybe a month ago I'd be afraid of that, but not now. I know some things gotta change, son. Both with the diner and with life in general. Like this." He held up the tablet, speaking for him. "But we adapt and do what we gotta do."

Jack nodded, knowing it was true in a lot of ways.

And that life change in general could spill over on Jack to topple his military dream.

But, today, the military hoopla felt more like a demand and a duty he dreaded, rather than the adrenaline-iced delight he'd always viewed it as before. Time spent with Dad and here back in his hometown with his employees were giving him a new sense of purpose.

Sully glared at the new healthy food the cafeteria delivery person had brought. "And look at that. I'll have to give up my greasy spoon beefy gravy for this godforsaken broccoli and this waterlogged cod."

Jack tried not to laugh. To be fair, the food looked fake. Except he knew it wasn't because Sully was shredding it to death with his fork as he lamented over his lost greasy gravy.

The cafeteria delivery person just winked at Jack and scurried out, good-soul smile intact.

"Do you're okay with us making some changes like this in the diner, Dad?"

Sully nodded. "One thing. Olivia's special to me. Got a daughterly place in my heart." His dad rested his hand on his own chest and then extended his hand to Jack as though passing the mantle. Jack tried not to stiffen. He didn't want Olivia in his heart. Or was it that he didn't want to admit she was already in there? "You promise to take good care of her for me until I get better."

Jack nodded. "I will."

"See that she gets proper rest, too. And if we can afford it, give the kid a big raise."

Jack couldn't bring himself to tell his dad they absolutely could not afford it. Jack had discovered that about when Dad spoke of "petty cash," he wasn't talking a thousand bucks like most small, family-owned businesses, but more like a hundred thousand. And about a third of that much was unaccounted for. Someone had taken it.

But he'd find a way to give Olivia what she deserved.

"She won't want special treatment, you understand. But she needs certain considerations. Be nice so she'll open up to you."

Jack smiled. His dad knew him pretty well, all things considered.

He might even know Jack's heart better than Jack did himself.

At the end of her shift later that week, Olivia knocked lightly on Sully's door. "Sully? You decent? It's Liver." While she waited, she grinned at the use of the nickname that would forever stick now because it made Sully smile.

"Why, yes, do come in, lass," she heard Sully's audio tablet say. He must have switched it to a Scottish accent. She'd heard he'd told the speech pathologist he wished the tablet had a Darth Vader voice so he could scare the night-shift nurses when they came tiptoeing around with their little penlights.

Grateful that Sully's sense of humor had survived the stroke, Olivia rounded the corner. She smiled at Jack, but that cold steely glint had returned to his eyes. What in the world?

Well, he'd be glad to hear her good news, then. "Guess what? My car is fixed. The mechanic is bringing it by here, with the keys. So you're cut loose from having to give me a ride, Jack."

She'd really grown to enjoy that time with him. But he apparently didn't feel the same. He didn't so much as blink before saying to Sully, "See? She shouldn't have bought a Chevy."

"I didn't buy it, actually. It was a gift. From your father." As soon as she blurted that out, she wanted to take the words back.

Sully lifted his tablet. "Make sure that car mechanic didn't charge you an arm and a leg, young lady."

"Jack said he'd cut me a deal."

"If Jack recommended him, then you'll be fine because that mechanic will know my son will skin him alive if he tried to take advantage of a lady. How much did it cost to fix the car, kiddo?"

"Not much," Olivia hedged, not wanting to make Sully feel bad that the car was a lemon. She loved the car. It's just that it wasn't always dependable, especially in colder weather. But she was grateful nonetheless.

She avoided eye contact with Jack, unsure if he even knew already that his dad had given the car to her. She'd tried to protest but Sully had insisted for a solid week before she gave in, with the caveat that he'd let her clean his house for a while. She'd still be doing it if Jack didn't live there now.

"How much is not much?" Sully asked through the audio tablet.

"A couple hundred is all," she fudged a little. It was closer to four hundred.

"You're a worse fibber than my son. Now you use that money I gave you at Christmastime to get that car fixed if need be, you hear?"

Jack's head whipped up. "What money?"

"None of your beeswax," Sully's tablet said to Jack.

Jack narrowed his eyes at Olivia. When the nurse came in to take Sully down to the occupational therapy lab, Jack rapidly approached Olivia, causing her to scramble back.

"How. Much." Jack's teeth were gritted.

"A thousand dollars," she whispered hoarsely.

His jaw clenched. A gleam of warning in his eyes crushed the fragile bridge of trust they'd built.

She felt the fallout immediately.

But if this was all it took to obliterate their trust, maybe it hadn't meant as much to him as it had to her. Profound sadness came over her. And regret, for opening herself up to it…and to him.

"I tried to give it back. He wouldn't take it."

She felt helpless, knowing deep down he wasn't going to believe her, on that point or that she'd never asked for money. She could see it in his eyes. Looking at things from his perspective, she really couldn't blame him. She'd been secretive and cryptic.

"I often wonder, Olivia, how and why it is that you've become so close to my dad. Ever heard of elder abuse scammers? People who pretend to befriend the elderly people just to have a chance to con their way into their hearts and leave with their life savings?"

"I'd never, *ever* do that to your dad or to anyone." Her voice trembled. She leaned against the sink to regain her composure and to resist slapping Jack for saying that. She was thankful Sully was out of the room right now.

"First the car, then a thousand bucks, Olivia? What else have you taken from him?"

She opened her mouth to protest that she hadn't taken anything from Sully. However, maybe Jack considered her receiving Sully's gifts as taking. Especially if Sully couldn't afford to give them. For all Jack knew, his dad wasn't in a lucid frame of mind when he gave her those things. Even though Olivia felt he was. How could she convince him of her integrity?

"I can understand you being worried in the beginning about me using your father or taking advantage. But I thought you knew me better than that now." As hard as she tried, she couldn't keep the hurt out of her voice.

"So then you still have the money?"

"I—yes. Some of it." She couldn't tell him she'd paid the balance on the cost of the diner washer and dryer. Sully would find out and be heartbroken. She'd promised herself to spend it for an emergency or on school. She didn't want to hurt Sully by not using it for herself, but the diner needed those funds. And, technically, saving the diner was an emergency, right?

Olivia began to tremble at the look on Jack's face, the mistrust flooding back again.

"You had to know his faculties were failing when you accepted the gift," Jack accused.

"His faculties were fine up until a couple of days prior to his stroke. He was well before that. Believe what you want to." Done with this futile discussion and devastated beyond belief at the doubt arcing in his eyes, she turned to go.

He reached for her arm to turn her back. "I *want* to believe you, Olivia," he said. "But I need more to go on here."

"Like what?"

"Where's the rest of the money?"

She didn't want to tell him, but what choice did she have? Plus, maybe somehow his knowing would help. "If I tell you, you can't tell him."

Jack's eyebrows furrowed. "I'll be the judge of that."

"I made a promise to him, Jack. And I broke the promise."

"By blowing the money on stupid stuff."

He might as well have slapped her. "How dare you? When have you ever seen me spend frivolously? When?"

He gave her a blank look, then nodded. "You're right. I can't think of a single time."

"I am the anonymous donor who paid the rest of the washer and dryer fee."

Jack let her arm go. "What are you talking about?" He studied her, then tilted his head. "Wait, I never received the rest of the bill."

"Because I paid it that day in cash. The cash Sully gave me. The transaction is in the computer. The receipt is in the safe. Top shelf, right next to the tax documents for this year that I helped him sort through. Of course you probably think I cheated him on that, too."

At voices outside the door, Jack's hand went up. "Wait. He's back. We discuss this later."

The tech wheeled Sully in and helped him to his chair. Sully leaned over and made a face at his tablet. Then he punched the playback button and Olivia's heart felt as if it would stop.

"…I often wonder, Olivia, how and why it is that you've become so close to my dad. Ever heard of elder abuse scammers?'"

Sully's head wobbled up. "Who said that?"

Olivia put her face in her hands. "Oh, Sully…it's nothing, really."

"Don't seem like nothing to me," his audio tablet said. Sully's face grew red as he flared his nostrils at Jack. "What's this about, son? And don't try to lie to me. I may have had a stroke but I'm not brain-dead."

Sully wobbled to his feet. The therapist rushed to steady him. He fought the arms trying to get him to sit back down before he fell. He cast a concerned look Olivia's way and then glared holes through Jack. "Just what exactly are you accusing her of?"

Olivia's brain scrambled to cover for Jack in order to

calm Sully down. She searched Jack's face from across the room, trying to draw from his lead what to say to mend this.

Suddenly Jack surged forward, his face stricken. "Dad?"

Olivia whirled to find Sully's eyes rolling up into his head. His body began convulsing in his chair, and the room slid into chaos.

Chapter Eleven

"You're sure about this?" Jack asked the specialist who'd moved Sully back to the intensive care wing of EPTC for closer observation.

"Yes. I believe it was just a TIA, a ministroke this time, set off by emotional and physical stress. The therapist worked him pretty hard. I think it's too soon to be expecting so much of him. We need to rethink our long-term plan."

Jack sat, face in his hands. "This is my fault."

"I understand you had an argument in the room?"

"Well, that mimicking parrot of an electronic tablet gave us away, but, yeah. Right before he got back in there. Apparently its recording feature was on the voice-activated setting."

"Is the matter settled?"

"It will be. In fact, since he's stable and resting now, I need to go find Olivia and make it right."

"I believe one of the nurses directed her to the inner courtyard patio."

"Thanks. Call me if he changes."

"Will do."

Jack headed to the patio with images fresh in his mind

of Olivia fleeing the room as soon as Sully was stabilized. He'd never seen her so distraught.

And that was Jack's fault, too.

Remorse cut through him like flying shards of shrapnel as he navigated the corridors in search of the courtyard doors and the right words to say.

Midway down a glass-encased hallway, he saw a brick and ceramic mosaic fountain surrounded by shrubs and winter flowers. Huge decorative clay planters and pots dotted the perimeter and encased all sorts of greenery, with the three-tier water fountain as the centerpiece. The courtyard's carved octagon walls featured stained-glass images of hope and healing.

He pressed open the door and found himself instantly soothed by the water arcing over the eagle statue in the middle of the fountain. He heard murmuring on the other side and slowed his steps. There, through the rivulets of water, he could see Olivia pacing, hands pressed together tightly and against her mouth, as though praying. Back and forth she paced.

He approached, dreading the hurt he was about to see in her eyes, knowing he'd been the one to put it there. The terror on her face when his dad had collapsed had nearly collapsed her, too. But she'd kicked right in and helped the crew resuscitate his dad by handing them vital items and opening packages.

He followed the brick pattern of the courtyard around to where she paced. When she saw him, her steps stuttered before she paused, looking like she might go the other way to avoid him.

Jack picked up his pace to cut her off from fleeing. "Olivia, wait. Please. I came to apologize."

Her steps slowed. He stared at the stubborn set to her

stature, not blaming her for being defensive. He still had no idea what to say, how to apologize.

Father, I'm lost here. Give me the words.

As soon as he had the thought, a sense of true humility washed over him. He reached to rest a gentle hand on her shoulder. She stiffened at his touch. At first. He increased pressure of his hand in tender increments, until she turned.

"Is he okay?"

"He's resting well now."

She nodded, pressed a hand to her stomach and stared away. "Is he going to be okay?"

"Yes. You didn't need to leave."

"Yes. Yes, I did. You're right. I don't belong."

The hurt within her words cut Jack straight to the core.

In one strong, smooth motion, Jack pulled Olivia to him and held her close. "Yes, you do. You have every right to be by his side. I'm sorry. I never should have said that."

She softened then and stopped resisting Jack's embrace.

Her shoulders molded and melded into him and he felt her fight the surge of tears. Then moisture soaked the front of his shirt but he didn't care. She clung to Jack and Jack clung to her, both still trembling from Sully's episode in the room. Then she broke down, quaking shoulders, sobs, shuddering and all. "I was so scared, Jack. He turned so blue."

"That was scary. I know." Terrifying, if Jack were truthful. Sully had stopped breathing for nearly a minute but health-care workers had been able to revive him.

"I don't think I can do this," Olivia said. "Trauma care when it's someone I know."

"You handled yourself exceptionally in that emergency. You'll be a great paramedic."

She scoffed. "I can't even seem to get through EMT school."

"You will. Your grades are coming up, right?"

"Yes, but...only because of you helping me study and giving me grace with the schedule."

"You have what it takes, I promise you."

"I don't even care about that. I just want him to get better."

"I know. I think he will."

But not without significant life changes.

Jack recalled the doctor saying they needed to rethink Sully's long-term goals. And that meant that he might not be able to return to running the diner.

Jack had a big decision ahead. But with Olivia feeling so right in his arms, somehow the mountain didn't seem so impossible to scale.

After a pretty significant crying jag, during which Jack felt utterly inept, Olivia settled down and sniffled into Jack's chest.

He swallowed, not knowing what to say or do. "I've never seen you cry," he said.

An irritated scraping sound came out of her throat as she murmured, "Well, enjoy it while it lasts because you're never going to see it again."

Jack couldn't help it. It was so typical Olivia that he laughed.

To his joy, her tremulous mouth curved up in a smile, too.

After a moment of calm, still holding her, Jack said, "You're such a bright spot in Dad's life. I had no right to try and shove you out." He leaned back to tip her face up to his. "I am so very sorry, Olivia. Please forgive me?"

She nodded. Then she grinned up at him with a smile so staggeringly beautiful he couldn't help but smile back.

And somewhere between her smile and his, he forgot that he wasn't supposed to be falling in love with her.

Jack skimmed a gaze across her face, to her bright eyes and lovely mouth. *Lovely* mouth.

No more resisting. It was futile.

Jack lowered his face but paused a breath away, giving her a chance to be the one to come to her senses and stop this. Instead, she slid her hand up the rough edge of his jaw and blessed him with another sweet smile. Then she closed the distance between them.

He wasn't sure where she left off and where he started but the kiss was bliss. Within its ministrations, Jack felt his emotional barriers begin to melt away. She clung sweetly and more tightly, as though needing to glean strength from his embrace. He met her motion willingly, offering the strength and tender comfort she needed, only to discover that he needed it as much as she did, maybe more. Jack gave himself to the powerful current of emotion. Olivia responded in kind.

In the kiss's wake, Jack was pleased to discover Olivia's tears had stopped, blessedly replaced by joy in her bright eyes. And she was smiling. A smile he knew packed more power and danger than any explosive he could run across overseas. "Woman, you have me completely undone."

And he didn't regret it for an instant.

That amazing kiss began to restore every feeling he thought forever lost, obliterated in the ambush that had defused every emotion he'd ever had or been capable of.

In short, he'd started shutting down. He'd had to, to protect himself and to stay levelheaded. Unfortunately, the shutting down had never stopped. The massacre had left him lost in terms of how to feel, because he didn't want to feel at all. The pain was too much. The images too overpowering. But with help, and with God, and with a good woman at his side, he'd not only make it through, he'd overcome.

Looking into Olivia's eyes gave him reason enough to want to. To do more than just get through, more than just exist or survive. Jack wanted to be the man he saw in her eyes. He wanted to thrive.

He looked into her eyes and saw love.

Then the doubt crept in.

There was reality. The issue of his military standing. His unfinished business overseas.

Was he looking into the eyes of his new forever love? Or had God merely put Olivia in his path to prove to him that his emotions weren't gone forever after all?

Would he break her heart by loving then leaving?

How dare he indulge in a kiss when he couldn't confidently commit?

"Olivia, I—"

As though sensing his uncertainty, his impending apology, his war within, she slid her fingertips over his lips, then down to calm his heart. Slowly she shook her head, smiled in that way of hers and said, "Shhh, Jack. Don't ever be sorry for it. Not ever."

Never. Ever again. "This is your worst one yet," Olivia said to Patrice two weeks later and slid the experimental green-only-it's-orange smoothie back across the counter. "I'm sorry, but…no."

Patrice huffed. "What's wrong with avocados, cumin, oranges, carrots and pumpkin?"

"You lost me at cumin. Plus, it looks too much like the sawdusty stuff the elementary schools put down when kids lose their lunches. Blech."

Patrice giggled. "Party pooper." She slid the shake

back toward Olivia. "It tastes better than it looks. Come on, Chicken Little. Just one swallow."

When Patrice turned her back to check her phone as a text notification came through, Olivia used the opportunity to rush the hideous drink to the sink. She tilted the equivalent of ten gulps down the disposal and tossed orange peelings over it to hide the evidence.

"I saw that." Patrice sipped her shake while one-thumbing a message back to whomever had texted her.

Olivia rolled her eyes, wondering when Patrice's strange shake-ology spree would end.

Patrice's phone *bleeped* another incoming text.

"Your honey called a crew meeting. Check your messages."

Pleasure rushed through Olivia at the thought of Jack. She checked her phone. "Nada." Why hadn't he texted Olivia? They'd been talking constantly, all week, and had been since their courtyard kiss.

Patrice lowered her legs from the stool next to the one on which she was seated. "Huh. That's weird. He seemed okay this weekend hanging out with the diner gang."

"Yeah." Olivia was thankful Jack had started doing things with the crew. That was a big step for him. Something occurred to Olivia. "He received a phone call from his military superiors late yesterday and seemed troubled ever since."

Olivia had given him space, but now she was getting concerned. "When's the meeting?"

Patrice stood. "This morning before shift opening, if possible." Her brows furrowed. "Must be an emergency for him to give no notice."

"Must be." Olivia thought of his phone call. A bad feeling went through her.

Jack had shared with her about the mission he'd been

given the opportunity to head. His superiors were simply waiting for more intel to give it a go.

Had that intel arrived? And…would Jack be leaving sooner rather than later?

On the way downstairs to the diner, Patrice asked Olivia, "How's Sully doing?"

"Better than expected." Not only had he been moved out of ICU and back to the rehab wing, doctors were optimistic he'd get to come home in the next few weeks. Things were definitely looking up there, as well as at school. She couldn't wait to tell Jack she'd aced her EMT final. After helping her study the day after their kiss, he'd joined the day-shift crew at a local play in the park, put on by members of her congregation—and Jack's, now that he'd begun visiting church with her. Unfortunately, the play had been a princess-and-the-frog parody called *Their First Kiss* and Olivia had felt Jack's eyes and grin on her the entire time.

Other than Patrice, no one knew about the courtyard kiss. They hadn't repeated it, but they had talked about it. She and Jack had decided that, while they both agreed that the emotion of Sully's situation drove them to the kiss, neither regretted it and they acknowledged something between them of substance.

Jack had called it love.

Olivia wasn't so sure.

She just knew she didn't regret the moment and all it meant. It mattered to her especially because of the healing impact it seemed to have on Jack, now in counseling for post-traumatic stress over the combat-related events he'd disclosed the evening of their kiss. Unimaginable things he'd endured while serving his country. That he was willing to walk right back into that level of danger and trauma spoke of his duty-bound dedication to the greater good. And convinced her that he'd come out the other side of that ambush with his character intact, despite the fact that his emotions had been left smoldering in the sand.

When they got downstairs, Jack was out back helping Naem, Darin and Tristan, the new dishwasher, unload a delivery truck.

Patrice brought Olivia into the office to show her a note Jack attached to the front edge of his Ford license plate poster in such a manner that the text read *Olivia loves Jack's...* Ford.

"I'm going to kill him."

"Hate the truck, but love the man."

"I do love him. I do not choose to love that truck." She laughed, surprising even herself by admitting it aloud.

"So, you really do love him?" Patrice beamed at the possibility.

"Don't overreact. The future is too unsure for us to do anything serious about it."

Patrice sighed. "I knew you two were falling."

"To me, a person doesn't fall into love. They choose to love."

To Olivia, love wasn't as much of an emotion as it was a conscious decision. Because emotions could be battered and they could wax and wane, whereas choices, at least hers, remained, no matter what fickle tricks emotions pulled.

"I can't believe he asked you out, to be his girlfriend exclusively and you turned him down," Patrice scolded Olivia.

"I can't commit until I have my EMT license and a job. You know that. It's what I've always said."

"And what if he returns to duty? What then?"

"Then if it's meant to be, God will bring him back to me."

Patrice sighed again. "I can't decide if that's romantic or pathetic. So let's go with romantic." A text came in on her phone. She eyed it and shook her head, then accidentally filled the sugar container all the way up.

"Shoot. Jack's going to come unglued."

"No, he won't," Olivia said. "I have firsthand knowledge that in today's staff meeting, Jack is going to remove the mandate to only fill them half full."

"Just how did you manage that?"

She smirked. "One day when we were slammed, I put him in charge of refilling all of the empty condiment containers halfway. He got sick of it and so now he's changing it back to filling them all up."

Patrice laughed. "Figures. When it's him doing unnecessary work…"

Olivia felt Jack before she saw him. Every other day when he'd approached, his arms had discreetly curved around her waist and he'd planted a kiss on the back of her head. Today, he just stood behind her. Patrice cleared her throat and left to get the seating area ready to open.

Olivia turned around trying to summon peace but feeling dread. One look in Jack's eyes and she knew. "You're leaving."

Something flickered in his eyes. "It looks that way."

There was a part of her that wanted to ask him to stay, and she thought maybe he wanted that too. But she could not. She would not be the cause of derailing his dreams.

Tears pricked her eyes. She quickly turned. "I need to help Patrice."

Jack moved quickly, his hand on her arm. Their gazes locked, but Olivia forced herself to look away. Then slowly she eased from the power of his tender touch.

He seemed at first to start after her, but something stopped him. The hitch in his breathing and the conflicted look on his face left an empty feeling inside her. All their memories and moments flashed in in her mind as her vision was blurred by tears.

The only way to keep from running back to him was to forge ahead.

And so she did, despite that her heart shredded more with every step.

God, give me strength to do this. I don't want to be the one to hold him back.

Nor did she want her own dreams to die over love that gave no guarantee. But one look back over her shoulder to find his eyes still fastened on her and she realized she'd rather run back to him and be held, than to be held back.

Instead of breaking through the fear that swirled around her, she kept walking, away from him.

Lord, if this is meant to be, bring it back to me.

Chapter Twelve

"Where's Patrice?" Jack asked Marci, the new hostess Olivia had trained.

Marci indicated the spoon-and-fork-themed wall clock. "She hasn't come back from lunch yet."

Olivia stood up from where she stacked trays behind the customer order counter. "Really? That's weird. She's never late returning."

The concern on her face made the hair stand up on the back of Jack's neck. He met Olivia's dark and troubled eyes. It was the first time in two weeks that she'd bothered to hold his gaze. "Call her. Make sure she's okay."

He hadn't meant to come across as bossy, but he had a meeting in ten minutes with prospective buyers for the diner. Then he had to work on finding Dad an apartment that didn't involve climbing stairs.

It suddenly hit Jack that he'd need to tell Olivia and Patrice there was a possibility the diner's possible new owners may not want the upstairs to remain rental units.

Which would mean they'd have to move, and maybe quickly.

If Patrice was okay. She'd been slow in following advice from her doctor and counselor to get away from Frankie and press charges.

"No answer," Olivia said, holding up her phone. "Marci, cover my tables. I'm going to go look for Patr—" Olivia was saying just as the door bells jingled and Patrice stumbled in crying.

Marci covered the dining room while Jack and Olivia ushered a sobbing Patrice back to the office and closed the door. They helped her sit but she sprang up, arms thrashing. "He's cheating on me."

"How do you know?"

"I caught him."

Olivia handed Patrice a handful of tissues.

"I tried to call him to tell him I wouldn't be able to make the dinner party tonight, after all, but he didn't answer. His voice mail was full and I wasn't able to leave a message. So I decided to go to his law firm and tell him in person. The secretary wasn't at her desk." Her words came out in huge hiccuping sobs. "I went to his office. Only when I pushed the door open, she—she—she was on his lap and—well, they certainly weren't working. How could he do this to me?"

"I'm so sorry. What did you do?"

"I turned around and left. Then vomited in the parking lot. I heard him calling across the lot and knew he'd be coming to try and make some excuse, but I know what I saw. There was no mistaking what was going on. I took off and he started yelling at me and chasing my car."

"I'm actually impressed," Jack said wryly, "that you didn't opt to run over him."

Patrice snorted. "Oh, trust me, I thought about it. But he's not worth doing hard time. I'm done with him. Why didn't I listen to you all before now?"

No one really wanted to answer that, as evidenced by the silence.

"You need to watch your back, Patrice. Don't go anywhere alone," Olivia said.

"I'm sure Darin would be willing to be your bodyguard," Jack said.

Olivia saw where Jack was going with this and recalled a conversation in which Darin admitted to having feelings for Patrice. Obviously Jack wasn't above matchmaking in addition to ensuring protection for Patrice.

"Yeah, and since Darin doesn't have his license, you could swap rides for his company and companionship," Olivia added conspicuously.

"I wouldn't want to put him out. Darin has his own life."

Olivia peered at Patrice thoughtfully. "I'm quite sure he wouldn't mind."

She looked from Jack to Olivia. "Why do I get the feeling there's something brewing here that you're not telling me?" Her eyes widened. "Darin's not, he's not interested in me, is he?"

Jack's eyebrows lifted. "For someone so smart, you can act dense."

Patrice blinked twice, then looked hopeful for the first time in ages. Olivia met Jack's amused gaze and smiled.

Marel poked her head in. "Egg substitute and turkey bacon for Mayor Whiffler's wife?"

Olivia sank lower in her chair as Jack turned around to stare at her. "You're still catering to her complaints about our not having healthy meals?"

"She's the only citizen in Eagle Point who cares enough to complain about Sully's greasy spoon. So, yes, we went against your directives and keep turkey bacon and egg white mixture in the fridge for her...and the few other customers who happen to come in with their doctors, nutritionists or Pilates instructors already in the dining room. Otherwise, it's great gobs of grease for all. Really, Jack, you should consider a healthy alternative menu."

"That, or let us carry clot busters on the condiment cart," Patrice quipped.

Jack shook his head.

"You look exactly like your dad when you do that."

"Speaking of Dad, I need to call about the assisted-living place."

Olivia's face blanched, as though it were becoming real that Jack was leaving.

He'd barely come to grips with it himself. In fact, his impending departure felt surreal. He'd been unsettled since making the decision. But who could blame him? So much had changed. Dad's stroke, falling in love with Olivia, the battle to save the diner…

Jack sighed and tried to shift his thoughts out from underneath the melancholy cloud. "Carry on."

After making phone calls, he checked to see if Darin needed help. "I'm guessing you're wondering about Patrice. Did you hear any of it?" The walls were thin enough to allow for that, unfortunately.

"Some. Just that he cheated on her. If that's what it took to get her to dump him, then maybe her walking in on that mess was a blessing in disguise." Darin shook his head. "Although I hate that she had to endure it."

"Maybe you can help her through. Hang out with her. Be a friend."

"She's above me, man."

"What makes you say that?"

"Look at me? I'm a tatted-up ex-con from the wrong side of the tracks."

"You did time for someone else's crime and you were exonerated."

"Yeah, but my incarceration still follows me like a black cloud. Plus, I did make some bad choices that got me in some bad places."

"Your past doesn't have the last word, Darin, God does. I challenge you to believe the best is yet to come."

Olivia stood by the condiment cart listening in awe. When Jack stepped away, she resisted the urge to brush a hand along his broad back and tell him how proud of him she was. If she touched him, she'd cave in her resolve to let him make his own choice about leaving.

When Jack stepped into his office and closed the door, Olivia walked up to Darin. "Never thought I'd say this but Jack is right, you know."

Darin looked at her. "You think so?"

She nodded. "I do. You're not disqualified. I know you trust in Jesus, and I know He knows that. So there's no way you'll be put to shame."

"Yeah, but she's so classy and her ex-boyfriend is all cultured and stuff."

Olivia snorted. "Sour milk is cultured, but that doesn't mean it's good for her."

Darin nodded. "Noted."

Just then, the door opened and Patrice's boyfriend, Frankie, stepped through the front door of Sully's dining room with a vengeful glint in his eyes.

Darin knocked hard on Jack's door. Naem paused and pulled a pen out from behind his ear as Jack stepped into the hallway.

"Jack." Olivia nodded toward the entrance. Immediately Jack transformed, marching toward the front like a man on a lethal mission.

"Oh my," Marci said, squeezing Olivia's arm. "The syrup's about to hit the fan."

Naem blinked at her oddly. "Syrup wouldn't spray, though."

Marci rolled her eyes and snapped her gum at him before going to refill patrons' drinks.

"Darin." Olivia put a calming hand on his arm. His biceps and triceps were flexing.

Naem nudged Darin aside and took over the grill so the meat wouldn't burn. "Go make sure Jack doesn't take the dude's head off."

"You mean beat him to it?"

Naem paused. "He's not worth getting sent back down. Just remember to be diplomatic."

"I know for a fact that no-good creep left bruises on her. And you want me to throw down diplomacy? I don't think so."

Patrice stood in front of Darin. "Actually Naem, why don't *you* go help Jack. Darin needs to stay on the grills."

Muscles bunching, Darin took the spatula back from Naem and muttered, "He comes in here again, and I promise you, he won't walk out." He rotated his neck and winked at Olivia. "At least not without crutches."

Olivia nibbled her lip, glad to see Darin cooling and able to kid a little. She really didn't want him violating his good standing with his parole officer. He was almost finished and didn't need the setback.

Olivia followed Naem to where Jack stood in front of the register glaring across the tables at Frankie, who'd sat down at a table.

"Why isn't Jack making him leave?" Marci asked.

"Probably because, legally, he can't." He could stare Frankie through the floor though, and that's exactly what Jack appeared to be trying to do.

"Take a picture, Sullenberger, it'll last longer," Frankie finally chided. He peeled open a menu and smirked.

Jack stalked over, slammed the menu shut and leaned into Frankie's face. "Outside. Now."

Frankie didn't even blink. "I'm fine right here, thanks." His tone was as menacing as his expression.

Patrice rushed out, having witnessed the exchange from the kitchen doorway. "He's a big chicken, Jack. He won't go to the alley to talk to you." She raised her voice, for other patrons to hear. "In fact, he only picks on people he knows he can beat. Like women half his size."

Frankie narrowed his gaze and darted a look around. "Shut your mouth," he snapped at Patrice.

She began rolling her sleeves up, bringing new bruises to light. "Shall we show everyone what you do in your spare time?"

His face reddened as he stood. "Fine." He faced Jack. "But you lay one finger on me and I swear I'll sue you and your dad and this diner for everything you've got."

Frankie stepped out and headed for the door, and Jack followed.

Almost too calmly.

"We should call the police," Olivia said to Marci.

"Why? If we do, they'll take Jack to jail when he beats the crud out of Frankie. My bet's on Jack."

Patrice gasped. "Marci!"

Olivia shook her head and gave Marci a look.

"Oh. Right. I'll just phone the police, then." Marci grabbed the cordless and dialed.

Olivia grabbed pepper spray out of her purse and followed Jack to the alley.

He had stellar self-control, that's all she knew.

Naem rushed ahead to intercept Jack. "Gonna beat her boyfriend into juice, boss?"

Olivia approached rapidly.

Jack's jaw just clenched. "Olivia, stay inside."

She screeched to a halt. She peered at Jack's muscular bulk and enormous bare hands, then at her pathetic little pepper spray and realized that he could probably kill four men in the ten minutes it would take her to figure out how to get the stupid safety off the pepper spray. It was probably expired, anyway.

Five minutes later, Olivia could stand it no longer. "I'm going to check."

"Not without a bodyguard you aren't," Darin said.

As they approached, Frankie was up against the wall and Jack stood an easy inch away from him.

Jack looked a deadly kind of calm.

Frankie spat on the ground near Jack's feet. "Are you still talking?"

Jack stepped closer, his hand near Frankie's neck on the brick wall. "Are you still breathing? Because if so, I can take care of that in about two seconds."

A policeman pulled into the alley and exited his car. "Jack, step away. Let us handle it."

Jack nodded to the officers and then scowled when he saw Olivia.

"You don't listen very well," Jack said, motioning her inside. He seemed calmer than before.

"Frankie's in one piece. I'm surprised."

"I took him outside to keep a ruckus from happening inside the diner. And to keep Darin off him."

"Good thinking."

Marci approached. "Jack, there's a man here who says he has an appointment to look at the diner."

Jack cast a glance at Olivia then looked away. "Direct him to my office."

Olivia froze. "Look at the diner for what? Is something being repaired?"

The expression on Jack's face stopped her in her tracks. "No. Nothing's being repaired." He turned to walk down the hall to his office.

She followed, a burning sensation dropping into her stomach. "Jack…what's this diner meeting about?"

"None of your business, Olivia."

"So, I'm not a part of your decision making just because we have to postpone having a life together?"

"Tomorrow is never promised."

Her face must've reflected her hurt because Jack glanced back and softened his expression. "Look, that came out wrong. We'll talk about us later. I can't miss this meeting."

"Can I know what it's about?" she asked, willing the panic away.

"Why? You'll just try to change my mind."

"About what?"

"Selling the diner."

She rushed around and stood in his path, not caring that the man he was meeting with was walking toward them, escorted by Marci, since Patrice followed officers to finally press charges against Frankie. "You can't sell the diner."

"Why not?"

"Because that would break your dad's heart."

"He'll be fine."

"No."

Did she just stomp? Really?

She must have because Jack's gaze dropped to her foot and his eyebrows rose.

Mature, Olivia. Real mature!

She drew a calming breath. "It would break his spirit and make him give up."

Jack motioned for Marci to take the man on in, while Jack mumbled an apology to him.

Olivia stood like a human blockade in front of the door. *As if* that would help. "What else does he have to live for, Jack, if not you and the diner? If you sell it, you'll be gone in a flash back to your life and you're all he has. He's all you have. You need to keep the diner. Please. I am begging you…"

"Olivia, I don't have a choice. The bank is foreclosing at the end of the month. We're done here."

We're done here.

She gasped. It felt like he'd ripped her heart right out of her chest. "Jack."

"I've done what I can. I'm sorry."

Which meant that by the time this mystery man left today, the selling of the diner would be a done deal.

Olivia stood staring at the walls, the war memorabilia, the decades of Sullenberger history. The photos grew blurry but she blinked back tears.

She pressed hands to the walls, steadying her breaths, her thoughts and her faith.

I will not let him do this, Lord. Not to himself. Not to his dad. Not to me. I want him here. I want a life with him. Help me stop him.

Maybe all along what he'd needed was the one thing she'd not been able or fully willing to give him.

A reason to stay.

Chapter Thirteen

"Olivia, I need to talk to you."

Patrice pulled the covers back from Olivia as she lay in her bed, then tugged on the sleeve of Olivia's worn Scooby-Doo pajamas.

Olivia squinted at her clock. Two in the morning. "Can it wait?"

"No. Now."

Patrice's eyes filled with tears and she'd apparently already cried all of her mascara off.

Fully awake now, Olivia swung her feet around and stood, grabbing her robe. "Where have you been?"

"At the police station. Frankie has been arrested for the time being." Patrice hesitated for a moment, and then continued. "I turned myself in, too, but they let me go because I cooperated."

Turned herself in? What did that mean? "Patrice... what are you saying?"

"Jack will hate me. Sully will never forgive me. He'll have another stroke. I've been so stupid." Patrice was near hyperventilation as she paced the hallway between her bedroom and Olivia's.

An anchor of dread dropped into Olivia's stomach, making movement hard.

She forced herself forward, drawing Patrice into the living room with her as she went.

Patrice nodded toward their apartment door. "Get Jack."

Olivia tied her robe belt. "You're sure?"

"Yes. He needs to hear this." Patrice clutched her stomach. "It's about…the money."

Bad feeling worsening, Olivia rushed across the hall and knocked frantically on his door.

He came out in his gym shorts and T-shirt looking as groggy, cranky and confused as Olivia had felt about a minute ago.

"Jack, Patrice needs to talk to us."

He scrubbed a hand across his face. Olivia tried to ignore the very appealing shadow of scruff along his jaw.

He twisted his wrist to peer at his watch. "At two in the morning?"

Olivia clutched her own stomach and shifted from one foot to the other. She hated to say this. She really, really did. "Jack, I think it has to do with the missing diner money."

Jack jerked instantly awake.

He spun, grabbed a sweatshirt and motioned Olivia back across the hall. They entered the girls' apartment one after the other. Jack helped Olivia drag chairs over.

She'd never forget the deeply disturbed look on his face. Truthfully, she felt just as troubled.

"What's going on?" he asked Patrice while turning a chair around across from her and straddling it.

He was surprisingly calm in this crisis. Maybe it was a God thing. Reading his Bible had really helped him.

It gave Olivia hope he'd stay safe overseas, in whatever situation he was stepping into in Syria.

Olivia sat in the chair Jack had situated for her between his and Patrice's, forming an intimate circle. She began silently praying as Patrice rocked back and forth, seemingly terrified to speak. Jack waited.

After a long tense moment, Patrice moved her gaze up to his and Olivia's briefly before settling it back on the floor. "I'm sorry. I'm having a hard time."

"Just start from the beginning."

Patrice finally took a brave breath and started.

"A few months after I started dating Frankie, I discovered he had a cocaine habit. I threatened to leave him and he told me he'd kick it. I stupidly believed him. He either quit for a while or, more likely, he just hid the habit well."

Jack scrubbed a hand over his face but appeared to reinforce his will to listen patiently.

"A few months later he had me borrow money from Sully's safe, to pay some people off. I thought it was for some personal loans because that's what he told me. But then I heard him bragging recently that he'd snowed me and Sully out of sniff money…and I knew that he'd never quit the cocaine."

Olivia took a look at Jack, who stared unbelievingly toward the wall.

Patrice twisted in her seat and choked back a sob. "Every dime of Sully's safe money went right up Frankie's nose. It was a lot of money."

Jack's jaw was clenching, but he still sounded remarkably calm. "Would you be willing to testify?"

"Yes. I've already gone to the police. They took a statement and since one of them knows me and is your good friend, Jack, he told me to come straight to you and to tell you everything. He said you can come back to the station anytime today to give a formal statement to at-test to the missing funds."

"How much money are we talking about here?" Jack looked from Olivia to Patrice.

"Forty-five thousand dollars."

Jack felt like hitting something.

"Wait, Jack. That may be enough to get the diner out of the red."

"No. It's not. We'd still be thirty thousand dollars short, and we can't make that in six days."

"I'm so sorry, Jack. He promised to pay it back. But he never did. He kept making some excuse. I didn't re-alize the diner was in danger of shutting down. I didn't know what to do. I deserve to go to jail. I know I do."

"I'm not going to press charges against you, Patrice. Just Frankie. But please show me that you have learned from this."

"I have. I promise. I've been putting every dime of my tips in to try to make up for it."

"That makes two of you," Jack said, looking at Olivia.

"You know about that?"

"It wasn't too hard to figure out once I started count-ing the register before and after you came on shift."

Olivia dipped her head.

"His law firm is doing well financially. Could you be compensated that way?" Patrice asked.

Jack's jaw clenched. "Doubtful."

"What are you going to do, Jack?" Olivia asked.

"I'm going to let the police do their job investigating to prove his guilt."

That didn't mean he'd ever recover Dad's money.

Jack felt literally sick to his stomach, a rarity. His head ached to a point where his brain felt squeezed.

Jack made the phone call, despite that it was closing in on three in the morning. As Jack explained the situation to a detective named Ashleigh Petrowski, he realized he still hadn't gotten over the great shock of Patrice's actions.

He knew she was remorseful, but he never dreamed she'd be capable of something like this. He shook it off, choosing to forgive and move ahead instead of spin his wheels and dwell.

Ashleigh told him she needed to consult with Stone, whoever that was, and she'd get back to him within the hour. While they waited, Jack, Olivia and Patrice went through two pots of coffee.

It was going to be a long, hard day.

Jack's phone rang somewhere around four in the morning. He spoke on conference call with Ashleigh, Stone and a federal agent who informed Jack that Frankie was already under investigation for another matter and that he was recording the call. Jack put Patrice on the phone next, to corroborate his story and give any details Jack didn't know or had inadvertently left out.

Afterward, Ashleigh brought Jack up to speed on what the plan would be from here. He rejoined Patrice and Olivia in the living room. Olivia had showered and dressed. Patrice still looked like she'd been on a three-day bender, only he knew she didn't indulge.

He explained to them, "Ash can get FBI wired and meet up with Frankie in a club, setting him up to brag about taking the money. Normally the FBI doesn't get involved in local police matters, but in this case, they were already investigating Frankie, with local law enforcement's assistance and knowledge. Looks like Frankie will be put away for at least a couple decades."

"Is Ash that skyscraper-tall blonde who looks like

a mix between a James Bond spy stunt woman and a Venice runway model? Wears Marilyn Monroe hair and drives a black Hummer?"

"That would be her."

"Oh, Frankie'd be all over that, believe me." Patrice rolled her eyes.

Jack studied Olivia, who appeared to squirm. She ought to know tall, leggy blondes were no longer his type.

His new and only type?

He was looking right at her.

He tried to catch her gaze, to smile and reassure her. But she avoided his eyes.

He fixed her another cup of coffee, just the way she liked it. Then he pulled up a chair next to her, letting his knee rest against hers. She may not have needed the contact but he did.

He felt relief when she didn't pull away.

"Thank you," she said, sipping her coffee.

After a moment, a gleam entered her eyes. "Jack, if we can raise the rest of the money, will you reconsider not selling the diner?"

Jack's gaze settled on Olivia. He reached over and threaded his fingers through hers. "The last thing I want to do is sell the diner. But I can't imagine raising that kind of dime in six days."

She squeezed his hand in return and turned that luminous smile on him. He could swear he forgot to breathe.

"Reminding you that God can do quite a bit in one week's time. You know, like create the whole wide world and everything in it?" she said.

Jack grinned. "Point taken. You have six days, Olivia. But don't keep me in the dark."

Chapter Fourteen

"You promised not to keep him in the dark," Patrice said to Olivia a week later.

"I never promised," she said while opening her trunk. "And since when do I always do what Jack tells me?"

"Since mostly never."

"Right. So, let's go over the plan again," Olivia said.

Patrice put the bolts of material from the donation center in her trunk. "We take this satin, velvet and lace to a woman who makes elaborate costumes for the fund-raiser ball. Local seamstresses will donate their time and people will buy the costumes. The money is being donated to the diner. Lauren, whom you trained under at EPTC, is the head seamstress. It was her idea."

So many things were coming together. Streams of revenue and rivers of generosity.

Olivia just hoped and prayed it would come through in time.

"Do you miss him, Olivia?"

Jack had flown to Washington, DC, for a four-day meeting with military officials about Syria. Something about tying up loose ends.

Patrice had suggested that perhaps Jack was there to

pass off his duties to someone else, so he could come home for good. Olivia wanted to believe that was true, but she felt selfish in doing so. Still, her heart yearned for it to be true. Jack had texted once but she hadn't heard from him after the first day.

Either he was forgetting about her, or he was up to something.

Patrice and Olivia headed for their daily visit to the assisted-living facility where Sully had been moved. He was enjoying it immensely because many of the residents were longtime diner patrons and old buddies. When they got there, Sully was working on a puzzle with a group of ladies. He wore his new voice-activated speech box around his neck. He had come a long way, but still needed help to regain all he'd lost. He hadn't lost his will or his spirit though, thankfully.

Patrice grinned. "He looks so happy here."

Olivia couldn't agree more.

Sully saw them and motioned them over. "Hey, my girls are here!"

At a swat from one of the elderly women at the table, Sully switched that to, "Errr, I mean my other girls. My daughter-like girls. Not my girlfriends."

Olivia grinned, knowing God had picked the perfect place for Sully to bloom in the next season of his life. As the ruckus started around the table, she studied the faces, the Bibles and the smiles, and gave thanks.

"Say, how'd you two pull off paying enough money to the bank to convince them to postpone foreclosure?"

Olivia was glad that Sully hadn't taken it too hard when Jack had had to tell him about the diner debt and how it had come about.

Sully continued, "The loan officer came by today to tell on you two." Tears filled his eyes. He didn't bother swiping them away, and his attempts to be scolding and surly just weren't very effective with the big grin that had taken over his face.

Olivia sat. "Word somehow got out that the diner needed help. All the people you and your family have helped over the years came through for you, Sully."

Patrice pulled up a chair on the other side of him. "Almost everyone in town's been coming to the diner multiple times a day. We can barely keep up."

"Even weirder, they all started paying triple on their meals, in addition to lavish tipping."

"Even the mayor's wife?" Sully's eyes bugged.

"Yep. I think she instigated a lot of it, in fact."

All week, businesses had been ordering their meals from the diner. Perry had even come back to work and he'd been a tremendous help and a blessing. It was clear he'd cleaned up, thanks to Jack.

"And the big news is that library owner Lem Bates asked me to tell you that he's donating the proceeds of this year's annual Library Storybook Ball to the diner."

"Oh, awesome! But, wait. The ball isn't until Saturday. We need the remaining money in two days."

"I've talked to the bank. They said if we can get ten percent of the remaining thirty thousand, they'll extend the deadline until after the Storybook Ball. They know Lem's good for it. With the help and support of the community, the ball raises gobs of money every year for different charities and causes."

"And the diner will be saved." Sully beamed.

Olivia nodded, joy bursting forth. "Looks like it."

Patrice blinked back tears and she hugged Sully. "I'm so sorry again. I can't say it enough."

"You have. You made a mistake, but you're making it right. I love you. Unconditionally."

She wrung her hands. "I don't know how you don't hate me."

Sully slung his arm over her shoulder and drew her nose to nose. "Because fathers don't hate their daughters. Now let it go and forgive yourself, like the Bible says."

Patrice hugged him and breathed pure relief, then said with a thankful voice, "I enjoyed church Sunday. I'm going to jump ahead of Jack and formally join."

With everything in chaos, he hadn't had a chance to officially join yet, but had been attending regularly with Olivia.

"He'll be right on your tail, trust me." Sully smacked at a resident who tried to nab one of the corner pieces Sully hoarded for the puzzle.

Olivia laughed.

Sully gazed at her in a fatherly manner. "And what about you and Jack?"

"I think I blew it."

"Oh, you didn't." Patrice patted Olivia's hand.

"He's barely talking to me."

"Maybe he's preparing to come home for good and make a life with you," Sully said out of the blue. Now why would he just up and say something like that?

A strange little twinkle lit Sully's eye before he winked at Patrice.

What was up with those two? Did they know something Olivia didn't?

The suspense was about to kill her. Unfortunately her doubt and fear were giving it a good run for its money.

"Or maybe he's trying to prepare to let go so he can go make a life without me for good."

"Olivia, have hope." Patrice hugged her.

"What should I do?"

"You said it yourself. Give him an irresistible reason to stay."

"I have the perfect idea," Sully announced. "Invite him to be your date at the ball."

"Yes, perfect!" Patrice clapped, then she grinned. "The theme for this year's Storybook Ball is Unlikely Allies."

If anything more accurately described Olivia and Jack and the bumpy beginning they'd shared, "unlikely allies" did.

Suddenly, she knew what she had to do.

"Fine. I'm texting him the invitation now." She practically broke out into a sweat doing so. He didn't answer, but he may not be able to if he was in a top-secret meeting or location. For once, Olivia chose faith over fear, despite the fact that she knew too much about being let down.

"He'll be home the day of the ball, his flight arrives two hours prior. Pray there are no delays."

Chapter Fifteen

Was he ever going to arrive?

After the third dance, the announcer said he had a local hero who wanted to say a few special words. Her heart sped, hoping…

Sully was grinning beside her.

"What?" Olivia shook her head at him.

Where was Jack? She checked her watch. His plane had been late. Was he okay?

"Olivia, look."

She looked up to see Jack walking up the steps of the stage. He looked so handsome dressed in Air Force blues that it took her breath away.

When he got onstage, everyone in the room stood to honor him and welcome him home.

With the help of new intel and his experience, he'd helped coordinate the capture of the insurgent who'd arranged the ambush on his unit, and Jack had been able to do so without stepping boots to the ground overseas. Olivia had not stopped thanking God since she'd heard the news.

Tears flooded her eyes and she wanted to rush up and take him down with a hug.

But this was a special moment. He was this year's guest of honor and he deserved it.

Smiling, she stood with the rest of the room looking at him with absolute adoration.

After receiving his award, Jack thanked everyone in Eagle Point and the surrounding communities for pulling together to save the diner. He then helped his dad onto the stage and Sully also received a standing ovation for stellar town service and sacrifice.

After the crowd calmed, Jack gazed across the room, directly into Olivia's eyes.

"I want to give a shout-out to a special lady here tonight. Olivia, can you come up here?"

Her heart began to pound as she rose to new applause and walked toward the stage. This was Jack's moment. Why was he sharing the spotlight with her?

She didn't like being the center of attention. Funny, considering all her tattoos and piercings.

Once she got to the stage, Jack took her hand and then he dropped to one knee, and produced a beautiful pewter and diamond ring—one with tiny elegant silver and black studs reflecting her rocker-girl flair.

Olivia gasped, completely blindsided.

He pushed the microphone away to make the moment intimate. A hush fell over the room. "Olivia, when I came back to Eagle Point, I only felt like half a man. You make me whole. I feel like you're the better part of me. You're the future I long to live for. Let's make it official. Let's make this love last forever. You know I love you, right?" he whispered.

"Yes. But what about your career?"

"I was miserable being away this week—from you, Dad, the hometown we love, the diner and even church. If I couldn't last four days, I knew I'd never survive another tour of duty without my heart leaving its post. So I knew it was time to retire. My honorable discharge went through this morning. I'm officially here for good."

"I'm so happy," she whispered, tears streaming down her cheeks.

"Will you make me the most thankful guy in creation? Will you marry me?"

She hugged him so hard he almost fell over. "I will! Oh, Jack. I love you so much! I got the better end of this deal!" she exclaimed to another round of clapping, cheers, whistles and applause.

Clearly, the audience figured out he'd proposed and she'd accepted. As they exited the stage, people came up to congratulate them, Sully among the first. They spoke at length with him, then endured teasing from the diner crew.

Then Jack tugged her hand and whispered as a romantic ballad came on, "Come share this moment with me."

After celebrating with a private dance on the light-strung patio under a sparkling array of stars, Jack led Olivia to the curb.

"Your carriage awaits, my love." His mouth twitched. "Unfortunately, they were out of Fords."

She saw the OFFICIAL CHEVY CARRIAGE…and burst out laughing, knowing the God of joy would hem them, two unlikely but loving allies, in between His guiding hands, all the days of their lives.

* * * * *

Dear Reader,

One of the toughest challenges I face as a storyteller is writing characters whose parents were abusive to or neglectful of them growing up. My parents were none of those things and the more I hear of the hardship some go through as a result of family dysfunction, the more I realize how fortunate I was in the parents God gave me. No parent or family is perfect of course, but I pray for you, dear reader, that no matter what, you know you have a place in the family of God. May you know His love and mercy, and know that there's hope for your future.

If you enjoyed spending time in fictional Eagle Point, other books in the series are listed on my website, cheryl wyatt.com, where you'll find order links, series lists and a newsletter sign-up for freebies, new book release news and other goodies exclusive to subscribers.

I love my readers and cherish interaction at facebook. com/CherylWyattAuthor. Hope to see you soon!

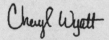

COMING NEXT MONTH FROM
Love Inspired®

Available February 16, 2016

A BABY FOR THE RANCHER
Lone Star Cowboy League • by Margaret Daley

Having discovered he's a father to a baby he never knew existed, bachelor Ben Stillwater seeks out a mother for his son. When Ben falls for pretty Lucy Benson, can he convince the busy sheriff to make room for a family?

THE RANCHER'S FIRST LOVE
Martin's Crossing • by Brenda Minton

Back in Martin's Crossing after ten years, Remington Jenkins realizes he's never forgotten the summer romance he once shared with Samantha Martin. Can he face her overprotective family once again and fight for a second chance at forever?

WRANGLING THE COWBOY'S HEART
Big Sky Cowboys • by Carolyne Aarsen

Jodie McCauley has agreed to stay at her late father's ranch until her wild horses are trained. Finding the perfect trainer leads her to Finn Hicks—the only man who's ever held her heart.

ACCIDENTAL DAD
Family Ties • by Lois Richer

Becoming the guardian of the twins his late brother hoped to adopt, rancher Sam Denver looks to the children's maternal aunt Kelly Krause for help. But when custody questions arise, they'll have to work together to keep their newly formed family intact.

THE LAWMAN'S SURPRISE FAMILY • by Patricia Johns

Police officer Ben Blake is shocked when high school sweetheart Sofia McCray returns home with a little boy she says is his son. After her newspaper job throws them together, Ben will prove he's the caring dad and husband Sofia seeks.

ALASKAN REUNION
Alaskan Grooms • by Belle Calhoune

Paige Reynolds is back in Love, Alaska, to rectify her late father's misdeeds—and introduce Cameron Prescott to the daughter she's kept hidden from him. Can Cameron forgive Paige and embrace a happily-ever-after with his first love?

LOOK FOR THESE AND OTHER LOVE INSPIRED BOOKS WHEREVER BOOKS ARE SOLD, INCLUDING MOST BOOKSTORES, SUPERMARKETS, DISCOUNT STORES AND DRUGSTORES.

LICNM0216

REQUEST YOUR FREE BOOKS!

2 FREE INSPIRATIONAL NOVELS
PLUS 2
FREE
MYSTERY GIFTS

Love Inspired®

YES! Please send me 2 FREE Love Inspired® novels and my 2 FREE mystery gifts (gifts are worth about $10). After receiving them, if I don't wish to receive any more books, I can return the shipping statement marked "cancel." If I don't cancel, I will receive 6 brand-new novels every month and be billed just $4.99 per book in the U.S. or $5.49 per book in Canada. That's a saving of at least 17% off the cover price. It's quite a bargain! Shipping and handling is just 50¢ per book in the U.S. and 75¢ per book in Canada.* I understand that accepting the 2 free books and gifts places me under no obligation to buy anything. I can always return a shipment and cancel at any time. Even if I never buy another book, the two free books and gifts are mine to keep forever.

105/305 IDN GH5P

Name	(PLEASE PRINT)	
Address		Apt. #
City	State/Prov.	Zip/Postal Code

Signature (if under 18, a parent or guardian must sign)

Mail to the **Reader Service**:
IN U.S.A.: P.O. Box 1867, Buffalo, NY 14240-1867
IN CANADA: P.O. Box 609, Fort Erie, Ontario L2A 5X3

**Are you a subscriber to Love Inspired® books
and want to receive the larger-print edition?
Call 1-800-873-8635 or visit www.ReaderService.com.**

* Terms and prices subject to change without notice. Prices do not include applicable taxes. Sales tax applicable in N.Y. Canadian residents will be charged applicable taxes. Offer not valid in Quebec. This offer is limited to one order per household. Not valid for current subscribers to Love Inspired books. All orders subject to credit approval. Credit or debit balances in a customer's account(s) may be offset by any other outstanding balance owed by or to the customer. Please allow 4 to 6 weeks for delivery. Offer available while quantities last.

Your Privacy—The Reader Service is committed to protecting your privacy. Our Privacy Policy is available online at www.ReaderService.com or upon request from the Reader Service.

We make a portion of our mailing list available to reputable third parties that offer products we believe may interest you. If you prefer that we not exchange your name with third parties, or if you wish to clarify or modify your communication preferences, please visit us at www.ReaderService.com/consumerschoice or write to us at Reader Service Preference Service, P.O. Box 9062, Buffalo, NY 14240-9062. Include your complete name and address.

LI15

When a woman's old love returns to town,
will she be able to resist his charms?

Read on for a sneak preview of
THE RANCHER'S FIRST LOVE
The next book in the series
MARTIN'S CROSSING

"What are you doing here?" she asked as she stretched. When she straightened, he was leaning against the side of his truck, watching her.

"I would have gone running with you if you'd called," he said.

She lifted one shoulder. "I like to run alone."

That was what had changed about her in the years since she'd been sent away. She'd gotten used to being alone.

"Of course." He sat on the tailgate of his truck. "I was driving through town and I saw you running. I didn't like the idea of leaving you here alone."

"I'm a big girl. No one needs to protect me or rescue me."

The words slipped out and she wished she'd kept quiet. Not that he would understand what she meant. He wouldn't guess that she'd waited for him to rescue her from her aunt Mavis, believing he'd show up and take her away.

But he hadn't rescued her. There hadn't been a letter or a phone call. Not once in all of those years had she ever heard from him.

"Sam?" The quiet, husky voice broke into her thoughts.

She faced the man who had broken her fifteen-year-old heart.

"Remington, I don't want to do this. I don't want to talk about what happened. I don't want to figure out the past. I'm building a future for myself. I have a job I love. I have a home, my family and a life I'm reclaiming. Don't make this about what happened before, because I don't want to go back."

He held up his hands in surrender. "I know. I promise, I'm here to talk about the future. Sit down, please."

"I don't want to sit."

"Stubborn as always." He grinned as he said it.

"Not stubborn. I just don't want to sit down."

"I'm sorry they sent you away," he said quietly. In the distance a train whistle echoed in the night. His words were soft, shifting things inside her that she didn't want shifted. Like the walls she'd built up around her.

"Me, too." She rubbed her hands down her arms. "I wasn't prepared to see you today."

She opened her mouth to tell him more but she couldn't. Not yet. Not tonight.

Don't miss
THE RANCHER'S FIRST LOVE by Brenda Minton
available March 2016 wherever
Love Inspired® books and ebooks are sold.

www.LoveInspired.com